K.O.'D
IN THE
VOLCANO

K.O.'d
in the Volcano

A K.O.'d in Hawai'i Mystery

by

For Deanna —
enjoy your "Big
trip to the
Isle"!

Mahalo —
Victoria

Victoria Heckman

PEMBERLEY

PEMBERLEY PRESS
PO Box 5840
Austin, Texas 78763-5840
www.pemberleypress.com

A member of The Authors Studio
www.theauthorsstudio.org

Cover design: kat & dog studios
Cover photo courtesy of:
T. Jane Takahashi
U.S. Geological Survey
Hawaiian Volcano Observatory
Photo of Victoria Heckman courtesy of:
Blue Moon Photography

Heckman, Victoria
K.O.'d in the Volcano
Library of Congress Control Number: 2003100193
ISBN: 0-9702727-5-8

First North American Edition
Printed in the United States of America
March 2003

For Hawai'i Volcanoes National Park,
and the spirit of Kalapana
—not only what
was lost, but what still remains.

In Memory of
Theresa from Molokai

Acknowledgements

This is a work of fiction, the characters and events based upon spirit and imagination. All errors are my own. While I have shamelessly rearranged Hawai'i Volcanoes National Park, not only physically but in NPS procedure, as well as the time frame of the Kalapana eruption phase, I have tried to remain true to the spirit of the Hawaiian people, to the spirit of those Hawaiian at heart, and to Madame Pele, Goddess of the Volcano.

Mahalo to Robb Kiaha and Leesah-Mari Kauwahionalani Tulafale for their invaluable assistance with Hawaiian language. Also, T. Jane Takahashi who so kindly provided the cover photo. Jane Kadohiro R.N., of the American Diabetes Association Youth Camps in Hawaii—my friend and mentor in diabetes care.

Thank you to my mom—Paula Farris, Sgt. Kathleen Osmond of HPD, Lt. Dennis Branahan, Ret. Chicago PD, Leona Evans and my Unity family, and Pat Ricks of Pemberley Press. I couldn't have done this without any one of you.

O ka la ko luna,
o ka pahoehoe ko lalo.

The sun above,
the smooth lava below.

CHAPTER ONE

Katrina "K.O." Ogden landed at Keahole Airport in Kona, Hawaiʻi. She loved the little airport with the landing strip carved right out of the black lava. Descending the plane's stairway to the tarmac, she inhaled deeply. Nothing else smelled like the Big Island. Scents of the ocean, jet fuel and plumeria blew in the warm breeze.

She walked the fifty feet to an open-air, tree-filled courtyard to hit the restrooms first. She never liked using the tiny bathrooms on the noisy prop-planes, and had managed to survive the forty-minute flight from her home on Oʻahu, despite chugging three Diet Pepsis.

Much relieved, she walked the few additional feet to baggage claim, another open-air pavilion with one carousel on each side—progress, since the days when baggage was just tossed out onto the runway next to the plane. Some of the other outer island airports were still like that. She sort of missed it.

The Big Island had always been one of K.O.'s favorite places in the islands, the true antithesis to the bustling city of Honolulu. As a Honolulu Police Officer, K.O.'s job in Records and Identification was to track data and minutiae for over a million people. K.O. herself lived on the far side of Oʻahu—the lush, peaceful windward side.

Thankfully, she had been granted a transfer, and upon her return from this working vacation, she would move with her chief clerk Selena Wade to Evidence—a move she anticipated with relish.

No security check—she hefted her large bag, and staggered towards the center curb to wait for the car rental courtesy bus. Once out of the shade, the sun was intense, and the sky seared the eyes with its blueness. Mauna Kea—a dormant volcano—soared above the airport, and disappeared into a grayish bank of vog— volcanic smog—that drifted from fifty miles away at Kilauea Caldera in the shadow of Mauna Loa.

K.O. saw that more new housing had worked its way up the mountain since her visit a year ago.

The Aloha Car Rentals courtesy van pulled up with a screech, and K.O. climbed into the blessed air-conditioned comfort before the driver could assist her. He loaded several bags for the tourists behind her.

As he pulled away from the curb and exited the small airport, he clicked on the microphone. "Aloha, everybody, my name is Kamuela, and welcome to the Big Island. We'll be at the Aloha Car Rentals office in just a few minutes, but if you have any questions, or if I can help out in any way, let me know."

K.O.'s blue-green eyes met Kamuela's brown ones in the rearview mirror. She could tell he smiled, because his eyes squinched up. She smiled back.

The van stopped at the office, and K.O. waited only a few minutes for her economy car. Translation: Don't rent this car if you're over 5'10", or have more than two bags. Fortunately, K.O.'s 5'7" fit comfortably, if not spaciously, into the driver's seat. Her large bag fit into the trunk, but her purse and carry-on had to ride inside with her.

Before she pulled out of the lot, she tuned the radio to a rock station, and cranked up both the stereo and the A/C. A short hop on the access road and she pulled out onto Highway 11, feeling that she was really on her way.

K.O. buzzed into Kona proper fifteen minutes later, and made a quick stop at the KTA grocery store for bottled water and a Snickers candy bar.

Her ultimate destination, the reason for her trip, was Hawai'i Volcanoes National Park, on the other side of the island. She had decided to fly into Keahole airport, visit a friend, and then enjoy the long drive to the park.

* * *

Marijuana plants, some over six feet tall, leafy and green, waved in the slight breeze on the slopes of Mauna Loa. Camouflaging the *pakalolo* were 'ohi'a trees, *maile* and bougainvillea.

A feral pig, tusks gleaming, nosed for roots at the boundary. He bumped a thin wire, and a blast echoed in the stillness. He screamed and ran as shotgun pellets fanned over his head to embed themselves in the tree trunks three feet above the ground. Then all was silent again in the dappled sunlight.

Two men and a woman pushed through the trees, stepped over the wire, and continued to the far side of the field. A small shack, roughly constructed and low to the ground, was their destination.

"Ho, Gerald!" the woman called as she entered the shack.

"Yeah, what?" Gerald answered, as he assessed the plants. Many were ready to harvest.

"What you t'ink of dis crop?"

"Yeah, brah," echoed the second man. "What you t'ink we going get for dem?"

"Tommy, relax already," Gerald said. "I don't know. Our job is just to cut 'em and haul 'em down da mountain. Rudy sells, and we just sit back and relax, have some beers, and count our money."

The woman, with long dark hair tied back, wearing a stained T-shirt and shorts, with hot pink rubber slippers on her feet, reappeared with three machetes. She handed the first to Gerald, who immediately began cutting the ripe plants.

The second she spun at the other man, who jumped out of the way. The machete landed point-down, quivering at his feet.

"Shit, Jolene, you tryin' to kill me, or what?"

"Yeah, or what, you *moke*. Jus' cut." Jolene strode to another section of the field and also began to work.

"Such a bitch, callin' me stupid." Tommy picked up the machete, but stood staring at Jolene.

Gerald sliced his way to the large Samoan. "Cheez, Tommy, we nevah gonna finish, you just stand there." A stripe of dirt crossed Gerald's forehead, and sweat ran across golden skin into his eyes.

"Gerald, you evah t'ink what it'd be like to save some plants jus' fo us? I mean, we do alla work, alla risk, and Rudy guys, they just make all da money."

"Tommy, don' talk like dat. You goin' get us busted. T'ings going da way dey s'posed to. Don't rock da boat."

Tommy's machete dangled loosely in his large hand. His blue "Hang Loose" T-shirt stretched tightly across his gut above his sarong, a wild blue and yellow print, that covered him from belly to ankles. He lowered his voice to a rumble.

"You ever tink about taking a little on da side?"

"What do you mean?"

"You know, we been bustin' ass for a year, and Jolene, she just hang around and make trouble. Just t'ink about it."

"No way, brah! You crazy? You been smokin' dis stuff instead of jus' cuttin' it? Jolene is Rudy's *cousin*, man. We gotta watch her. She's dangerous."

A muted thump, then Tommy pitched forward. A machete protruded from his back, a trickle of blood dampened his T-shirt. Jolene stood at the edge of the new growth.

Gerald's eyes grew wide. His heart hammered. "Oh, my God! You kill him? For what? You crazy?" His machete slithered out of his nerveless hand.

"Rudy tol' me Tommy was skimmin'. Tol' me to take care of it.

After what I jus' heard, this seemed the best way to take care of it."

She swayed up to Gerald, snaked her arms around his neck and ran her tongue over his unresisting lips. "Get ova it, Gerald. Don' wimp out on me now. On *us,* now. Rudy like make you one partner."

Gerald stared at Tommy's body.

Jolene's voice grew hard. "Do whatever you like, but if we don' get dis crop in, we both goin' be busted. Rudy don' like it late. We gotta dry it and get it to him for shipping." Jolene looked down at Tommy's body in disgust. "Da guy was such a pig. We canna carry him down da mountain. Shoots. Rudy goin' be pissed off I did it here. Now we canna use this field 'til his body gone. Da pigs and dogs can have him." Jolene wrenched her machete from Tommy's back, and marched back to the harvest. Gerald picked up his machete, and slowly followed, never taking his eyes from Jolene.

CHAPTER TWO

K.O. hoped to get her mind off her recent troubles, and the Big Island usually did the trick. Something about the air? The vog, probably. She smiled to herself. Some of her friends were really bothered by the sulphurous fumes that drifted overhead. Not K.O. Once she'd even hiked to the fresh lava flow, and it wasn't until an unexpected yellow cloud had completely enveloped her and the other tourists that she had felt a twinge of difficulty. She'd just held her breath and backed out of the cloud, which was soon dissipated by a brisk wind.

She turned the tiny car onto Mamalahoa Highway and began the ascent out of Kona towards Kainaliu and Captain Cook. Near Keahou, she pulled into a viewpoint, got out, and drank it in. Watercraft of all types, including a big gray battleship, dotted the distant horizon. The sun was straight overhead, and she felt the pangs of lunchtime hunger. Up this high, the humidity of lower Kona was absent, and a strong breeze whipped her red hair around her face.

She was pleased with her interim assignment, a working-vacation at Hawai'i Volcanoes National Park. At the request of the National Park Service, she had been hired to in-service park personnel in weapons, drugs, and self-defense, due to the rise in violent crimes in parks across the nation. As far as K.O. knew, HVNP hadn't experienced this rise, but her assignment indicated that the park service was at least taking precautions.

She reapplied sunscreen, sighed contentedly, and drove on towards one of her favorite restaurants along the cliff road that wound high above Kealakekua Bay.

K.O. had driven down the narrow, winding cut-off to the bay before. In fact, a friend lived right on the water across from Pu'u Honua *heiau*—place of refuge—but she wouldn't have time to visit her on this trip.

She passed Konawaena High school and the "Little Grass Shack" of the famous song, and started up the bay-front portion of the road.

Kealakekua Bay was a large bowl. The narrow, two-lane road curved mid-way up the side of the bowl, with steep cliffs above and below. Locals drove on it at two speeds, it seemed to K.O.— irritatingly slow, like the macadamia-nut-farm truck driver in front of her, or insanely fast like the guy wearing dark shades in the ratty black Datsun, who passed them both, going at least fifty miles an hour.

Unfamiliar with this upper road, K.O. drove at a moderate speed and passed the mac-nut truck at a relatively wide spot, but still, she was nervous. Hunger and relief surged through her when she spotted the dirt lot for the restaurant. She marveled at the structures above and below the road that clung to the cliffs by the grace of God, rather than by sound construction. Some of the buildings, including the restaurant, appeared to be at least fifty years old, but she was no judge—they could have been much older.

As she opened the wood-framed screen door, she noticed the ratty black Datsun, or its twin, parked on the other side of the building.

Delicious smells greeted her as she entered. She found a corner table and sat facing the door, as was her habit—to watch who came and went.

First order of business, the menu. Stashed between a small vase of flowers and the salt and pepper shakers, the laminated menu boasted an exotic mix of offerings. K.O. salivated as she dithered between pinto bean cakes with mango salsa, or a sautéed Portobello mushroom with feta cheese, Greek olives and couscous.

A young woman approached with a glass of ice water and smiled. "Ready yet?"

K.O. gulped half the water. "I think so." *Not really. What the hell.* "I'll have the pinto bean cakes and salsa *and* the Portobello mushroom, and a mango iced tea."

"Okee doke. Be right back."

And she was. She refilled K.O.'s water and set down a large glass of fragrant tea.

As K.O. waited, she people-watched, one of her favorite pastimes. Who looked like the ratty Datsun's driver? A man, she thought, but it could have been that rather masculine-looking female who sat at another table with a petite, feminine woman. *I guess it could be,* she mused, as she studied them. Suddenly, the masculine one turned and caught K.O. staring. She flipped K.O. off and scooted her chair closer to her date, putting one arm around her, and holding her hand.

Wow, she thinks I'm scoping her woman. She's giving me some major stink-eye. K.O., unintimidated, let her eyes rest on them a moment longer, then dismissed them, turning her chair towards the window where the beautiful mauka view of Mauna Loa rose, emerald and lush.

Her lunch arrived, and she ate every bite, savoring the exotic flavors and peaceful setting. The only downside was that she now had no room for the passion fruit cheesecake. Ah, another time.

She paid her bill and waddled back to her car. Her next stop was Ocean View, a small town reputed to be the largest subdivision in the United States. Nestled not far from South Point, the southernmost point in the U.S., even south of Mexico, it boasted cheap housing, large lots, and a comparatively large Caucasian population.

As she came out of "the curves," the windiest part of the road between Kona and Hilo, right in the heart of the Ka'u Desert, she couldn't wait to see her friend Jerry.

She passed the little road that led to the tiny fishing town of Milolii, right on the beach, and mile marker 88. She drove through bleak acres of past lava flows, some marked as recently as the 1960's. The road was repaved over the flow each time, she supposed, shivering at the thought of molten lava running under the road. Or worse, streaming down the mountain towards her and *over* the road. She shook her head to clear it of such scary thoughts, and again admired the landscape. The Manuka Forest Preserve, where she had stopped on a previous visit to use the public restroom and nearly been eaten alive by mosquitoes, whipped by on her left.

Not your average forest, she thought. It was true. No grass, but trees thrust out of the tumbled, jagged lava. Some seedlings, some forty or fifty feet tall, the beautiful *'ohi'a* stretched skyward. Slim, straight trunks, smooth barked, their branches started high up the tree, ending in bright red, bristling flowers.

She turned off the main highway at Aloha Drive and continued diagonally up the mountain to Jerry's house. The higher she went, the more tropical the vegetation became. Although Ocean View was considered a subdivision, it had none of the trappings of a traditional development. No streetlights. No sidewalks. No park. She'd heard a park was planned, but when she had passed the site a year ago, no ground had been broken. She supposed it was still like that—Hawaiian time dictated the pace.

She stopped in the middle of the little-used road to consult her map. No shoulder existed—just paved road, bordered by heaps of *a'a* lava, sharp and black, mixed with swirls of smooth *paho'eho'e* lava—nowhere to pull off, even if she wanted to.

True, the subdivision was a grid, but some Einstein had decided to cant the grid on the diagonal, with occasional up-down streets, like a pan of baklava slices—confusing to the visitor, to say the least.

Aha! She had passed the direct road, but if she went up the next, Paradise Parkway, she could find it.

To add to the navigational nightmare were the circles. Dotted throughout the grid were roads that circled an intersection of two roads. Jerry lived on one such circle.

Rats! She should have written specific directions when she'd confirmed her visit by phone. She had been sure then that she could find it by sight, but now, driving among identical piles of lava too high to see over or around, she wasn't so sure. She continued up Paradise Parkway, hoping to see something familiar. The terrain changed again from tropical to bleak, and the road dead-ended at the back of the Forest Preserve. She tried Outrigger Drive, pitted and unpaved, but it went up instead of down. Fog swirled around the car and she could see only a few feet past the windshield. She felt all alone at the top of the world. Mist stuck to the glass, and wipers were useless. She rolled down her window and stuck her head out.

It was so silent up here! The mist opened up briefly, and she gasped in dismay as a virtual moonscape spread before her.

I'd rather have the mist than look at that, she thought. Craters and mounds of lava, but not a sign of life; not even the hardy *'ohi'a.* She searched unsuccessfully for a wide place to turn around, then decided to inch the car in a three-point turn, rather than continue in the wrong direction. She couldn't read the street signs in the mist, anyway, even when there *was* one.

All I need is to drive off the road and pop a tire, or worse, break an axle, she thought. Sweat broke out on her forehead, and she grasped the wheel tightly as she edged towards sharp rock. She felt the front curb guard scrape, and stepped on the brake. Reversing, she again stuck her head out the window and carefully accelerated.

"Hey, what you doing here?" a deep male voice asked, about a foot from K.O.'s head.

Thoroughly startled, K.O. pressed the gas pedal, and lurched off the road into the lava. The engine stalled. One side of the car sank, and in panic, she thought she had surely ruptured a tire on the razor-sharp rock.

Trapped in the car, K.O. watched a figure loom towards her out of the mist. She twisted the key in the ignition. Nothing. She quickly pressed the raise window button, but nothing happened. The figure drew closer, and she frantically pressed again and again. The man put his hands on her open window frame and leaned in.

"So, you lost or what?" asked a nice-looking local man in a stained T-shirt and shorts.

K.O. caught her breath. She strained to think defensively and speak at the same time. "Yes, I am. A little. I'm trying to find my friend's house on Orchid, and I know I'm way too high."

"Yeah, you got that right." His golden skin looked sallow in the mist. In the low light, his slanted eyes and dark brows took on an evil cast as he eyed her slight frame. "You got a map or anyt'ing?"

"Um. Yes, right here." K.O. didn't want to turn away from him, but had to, in order to find the map. She glanced at the passenger seat. To her dismay, the map had slithered to the floor. She would be completely vulnerable when she reached for it. K.O. felt extremely *haole* at that moment. Usually, even in her work as a police officer, her race—her "whiteness"—didn't matter. Here, alone at the top of a volcano with a strange local man, she felt stirrings of—if not fear—at least, keen awareness of the chasm between Hawaiians and other races.

A dog barked nearby, and suddenly a large *poi* dog—a mongrel—poked dirty forepaws between the man's hands on the window, and the spell was broken.

"Hey, Hoku, you all dirty. Where you been?" The man pulled back from the window, and ruffled the dog's shaggy, black and white head. K.O. took that moment to grab the map. She realized that in her earlier panic, she had turned the engine off instead of on. She restarted the car.

"Here you go, sir. I really appreciate your help." K.O. handed him the map.

"Yeah, sure. No prob." He took the map and pointed with a dirt-encrusted finger to a section of streets. "'Kay, den. You here. You gotta go here." His finger trailed a simple line down Bamboo Lane and over Palm to Orchid. He mentioned a couple of landmarks to help K.O. find her way.

"Thanks a lot. I appreciate this. It's like the moon up here." At his look, she added, "But beautiful. Just isolated."

"We like it that way. That's why we live here." His tone was chillier.

"Yes, well. I'd better be going. I'm late as it is. Jerry's expecting me. Thanks again."

"Jerry? *Da kine* on Orchid Circle? That's your friend?" He was smiling now.

K.O. smiled slightly. "Yes, we've been friends for years. I knew him when he lived in Honolulu."

"Why didn't you say so? I just thought you were some *lolo* tourist! Jerry's friend. How 'bout that? Here, I give you a shove." He crossed in front of the car.

Oh, no. In her desire to escape, she had forgotten the tire. She leaned out again.

"Excuse me, but do I have a flat?"

"Nah, nah, nah, nah." He flapped his hands dismissing the idea. "Just in one hole. Step on the gas little bit, and I push."

Relief flooded K.O. She gently tapped the gas pedal, felt the tires grab and bump back onto the hardpack. She leaned out again. "Hey, thanks brah. I really mean it!"

"Anytime! What's your name, Jerry's friend?" He waved as she began to drive off.

"K.O.!" she shouted. "What's yours?"

"Darryl!" she thought he said.

Maybe Gerald, Merrill? Anyway, a nice guy. A lifesaver, in fact.

CHAPTER THREE

Jolene and Gerald finished the messy, exhausting job of cutting the *pakalolo*, carrying it to the truck, and hauling it to the drying station in a lava tube.

"Gerald? Gerald!" Jolene's voice, sharp and demanding, echoed through the tube. "Gerald, come look."

Gerald finished spreading mature plants across drying racks to his satisfaction, then joined Jolene in the second section of the tube.

Jolene had told him how she'd found this cave when she'd begun working for her cousin Rudy. He knew her family had lived in Pahala and hunted the lands between there and Hawai'i Volcanoes National Park, so she was familiar with the terrain, and nothing there had met her current need for hidden pot-growing. On a scouting trip outside her regular area, she had chanced upon this tube. Of varying sizes and mostly underground, lava tubes made perfect pre-fab homes for a variety of creatures, and she had marked it as a potential hiding place.

Since Tommy's sudden demise, the previous growing site was no longer viable, and she had already begun a seedling crop in the back portion of the tube. These plants were what now held her attention.

"Gerald. Why aren't these plants doing better?" Jolene stood, hands on hips, critically eyeing the young plants. Today she wore a print mini-dress, and her usual hot pink rubber slippers. Her hair hung down her slim back in a single dark braid.

Gerald squatted and poked a finger into the beds of transplanted soil, examined the Gro-lights, and felt the leaf texture. He stood and clapped the dirt from his hands.

"Different reasons. We have to make the growing conditions consistent. Some plants is too dry, others too wet. The Gro-lights hitting some plants more than others. Come on, I'll show you what to do."

For the next few hours, Gerald directed Jolene, and they drilled more drain holes in the large tubs of soil, adjusted lamps and watered plants.

All the water had to be carried in, since there were no water pipes to tap in this remote area. Rainfall was plentiful, but Jolene thought a catchment system would be visible from outside the tube, so she'd nixed that idea, saying she would rather haul the water herself. Some rainfall naturally seeped into the tube, and that was part of the problem. Solar powered Gro-lights with electrical lines snaking through puddles of water across the solid rock floor—smooth as poured concrete — gave inconsistent light and warmth. Gerald pounded hooks into the lava walls and hung as many lines as he could. Although at times the walls were wet too, this was the best solution he could offer.

Exhausted, Gerald and Jolene sat against the cold walls and drank Hawaiian Sun juice from her cooler.

"Now what?" Jolene demanded, once they'd rested a bit.

"What, what?"

"Babooze," she muttered. "Is it ready? Are we *pau*?"

"Yeah, we're done. For now. I real had it." He sighed.

"I'm tired too, but I'm ready to do whatever we need to keep this going." She gestured around her.

Gerald saw her set jaw and tensed form. "I going home. You just gotta watch the plants. I bring *da kine* tomorrow."

"What *da kine*?" Jolene sounded even more irritated.

"Plant thermometers. You stick 'em in the dirt, and they say like, how much water, how hot the plant. Like dat. So you don't over water or under water. Once you see how much water and light is best, we can make a system where we don't have to be here alla time."

"You so *poho*."

"*I* lazy! Look what I wen' did fo' you? I work my ass off!" Gerald's pidgin intensified. "You stupid, or what? You here every day, somebody goin' notice, bum bye, and you no like be here if dat happens, yeah?" Gerald stood. "Okay, dey find da plants, das one t'ing, but dey find *you,* das one noddah t'ing 'cause den dey find Rudy, and you dead fo' real!"

Jolene slowly stood. She brushed her dress off, snugged it down around her hips and walked to the cave entrance. "You're right." She stepped into the undergrowth and disappeared.

Gerald, still panting from his outburst, wondered if he'd just made a big mistake.

CHAPTER FOUR

K.O. drove her mini-rental car into Jerry's gravel drive. His small, square, green house sat facing the road, with the tumbled rock of the mountain rising behind it, ready to roll down and crush it at any moment.

She stepped past a row of old, red velvet-covered theatre seats on her way to the door. No response to her knock. She *was* late. Maybe he'd gone to the store—a small general store, post office, and a few other small businesses clustered along the road at the bottom of the development. That was always an adventure in Ocean View. However, any real shopping had to be done in Captain Cook, a forty-five minute drive west, or Kona, even farther. The only mall on the island was ninety miles east in Hilo. Serious shoppers did not live here.

K.O. went around the house and found Jerry—standing on his head, silent, and absolutely naked.

"Ho, Jerry, this some special welcome for me?" K.O. hollered.

Jerry opened his eyes, jumped to his feet and embraced her, oblivious to the sharp lava under his feet.

K.O. laughed and hugged him tight, not bothered in the slightest by his nakedness. His familiar smile warmed her as he wrapped flowered fabric around his hips. They sat on the edge of the deck, more like a wood patio, and she studied him.

More than a year had passed since she'd seen him. In his forties, but refusing to say where, he still had youthful features, sparkling eyes, and a mop of blondish hair that flopped rakishly over one eye. Yes, the hair was a little grayer than it had been, the skin a little more lined, but he seemed hale and hearty and boyish as ever.

He took her hand and held it. "So good to see you, K.O. I was wondering what happened to you! Fell in the volcano?"

"Nah, just my *haole* sense of direction! So, how are you? You look good."

"I am good. Things at the theatre are going well, but you know the politics and funding and everything."

"Yeah, I know. You been the Artistic Director how long now?"

"Three years."

"Still happy on the Big Island?"

"It's the best thing I've done. I was headed for a heart attack, directing and running the O'ahu Little Theatre. I've found such peace here." He breathed deeply and looked skyward.

K.O. followed his gaze, and saw several birds, clear blue sky—except for a tell-tale bank of vog to the east—and towering 'ohi'a trees. "So, seeing anyone special?" K.O. asked, squeezing his knee suggestively.

Jerry smiled and looked down. "Yeah."

"Yeah! All right! Tell."

"The last show we did, 'Moon Over Buffalo,' a new guy auditioned. We hit it off during rehearsals, and by opening, we were a couple!"

"Oh, honey, that's wonderful! I'm so happy for you!"

"Yes, it's been a dry spell."

"God, Jer. So, tell me all about him."

All that afternoon, they chatted in the comfortable way of old friends reunited. They moved to his living room sofa, and when dusk approached, K.O. rose and hugged her friend one last time.

"Oh, I meant to tell you, Jerry! I met a friend of yours up the mountain on some street in the subdivision."

"Who?"

"Remember I was late because I got lost? Well, Darryl or Merrill or somebody helped me out. I was a little worried, but when I mentioned your name, he got friendly. Kinda cute, too."

"What did he look like?"

"Local guy, T-shirt, shorts, slippers, you know. Long, dark hair, maybe hapa-Japanese, even."

Jerry pursed his lips while he walked her to her car. "I don't know. Doesn't ring any bells right now. I'll call you up at midnight when I remember!"

"Yeah, right. Anyway, you said you're directing a show at Volcanoes? So, you'll be around?"

"Yeah, we're doing 'Deathtrap.' Should be good. Rehearsals are in the arts complex by the museum and art gallery, not at Volcano House. The show opens in two weeks, so maybe you can see it?"

"I'm supposed to stay a week on the government's tab. But, I might have a special friend of my own visiting, so I may stay longer!"

"What, girlfriend! Tell!"

"Nope, you'll have to wait and see, just like I will!" K.O.'s eyes sparkled as she thought of Alani, the gorgeous brother of Lana, her friend and fellow police officer. Alani—tall, Hawaiian-Japanese, with longish dark hair, almond-shaped brown eyes, large hands, made strong by canoeing; she blushed as she thought of his muscular legs.

"What are you keeping from me! Who is this guy that makes you all giggly?" Jerry knuckle-rubbed the top of her head.

"It's something that just started last week. Well, not really. It probably started about seven years ago, but I never pursued it. I should say we re-met last week and the sparks sure flew on both sides."

Jerry leered, and K.O. laughed. "Stop it. You know what I mean. Anyway, I had to come here to train staff at Volcanoes National Park, and he said he might find a reason to visit his friends and relatives on the Big Island, too."

"Ooooh! K.O. might be gettin' some!"

"I should have known better than to tell you anything!" K.O. threw her hands up in mock frustration. "It's all very iffy. I'm here to work, but you know, if things should work out . . ."

"Okay, okay. So, back to me." Jerry put his hands on her shoulders. "Even if you're only here for a week, I still want you to see the show. You can come to one of the rehearsals during tech week, or a dress rehearsal, okay? And if you are staying, I want to meet your lov-ahhh!"

K.O. laughed helplessly. She loved Jerry for his sense of humor and overwhelming talent. "He's not my lover!"

"You say that now." Jerry pulled her close in a bone-cracking hug. "Better get going. The road's not so good at night until you get past Na'alehu, like around Pahala, remember."

"I remember, but thanks." They looked up as the familiar sound of helicopter rotors assaulted their ears.

"Boy, that's annoying. Happen often? Tourist choppers are really going far afield now, yeah?" An unmarked helicopter swooped over the mountain behind Jerry's house, following the dry tumble of boulders towards them. They could see two men in the cockpit, one with binocs.

"That's so low! They've got to be breaking some laws!" K.O. said indignantly. "What are they thinking? I can't even see the name of the tour company. Not very good advertising."

"That's not a tour, that's green harvest," Jerry said. They turned to watch the chopper as it banked out of sight.

"Oh, yeah. I forgot. Pot-spotting patrol. They ever get anyone around here? There's nowhere to hide it."

"You'd be surprised. A ten thousand dollar haul a few months ago, so they're still checking. People are sometimes kinda dumb around here, and I have to admit, this area has a rep for attracting the Mainland's poor white trash—present company excluded, of course."

K.O. laughed.

He opened her car door, helped her in, then slammed it shut. "I love you, girlfriend, you know."

"I know. I love you back, girlfriend."

Jerry smiled and waved until the road curved, and K.O. lost sight of him.

CHAPTER FIVE

Hawai'i Volcanoes Park Supervisory Ranger Melanie Ward had expected the HPD liaison already to have arrived. Now it was late afternoon—nearing dusk, in fact—and still no sign. She hoped nothing had happened. That would be all she needed after the latest incident.

Some tourists, careening down Chain of Craters Road to the active lava flow at the bottom, had gone off the pavement. Fortunately, the spot was one of the better they could have picked. A number of areas on the winding cliff road would have led to certain death after a high-speed plunge like theirs. They had suffered minor injuries, been taken to Hilo Hospital, then released.

Unlike last week. Park rangers at the lava flow access had tried to subdue an angry young man who wanted to cross the saw horse barriers that kept gawkers back from the dangerous, unstable lava at the ocean's edge. Unsure if the man had been drinking, Jodie and T.J. had detained him as he tried to drag his girlfriend unwillingly under the boards.

As they reported it later, he became more belligerent, shouting and swearing. T.J. laid a restraining arm on him, and Jodie called for back-up, but the man shoved the rangers away, yanked his girlfriend past the blockade, and dashed to the edge of the steaming black cliff.

A sulphur-yellow cloud of volcanic effluvia enveloped the couple, and a horrible grinding sound was pierced by a scream.

T.J. and Jodie pursued them, but had to stop when the cloud obscured their targets.

The cloud finally dissipated, pushed seaward by strong winds. As groups of tourists stood in horrified silence, Jody and T.J. clutched each other for support and carefully backed away from the newly-formed edge of a cliff that plunged straight into the roiling sea. Lava the size of a football field had broken off and been swallowed by the ocean, taking the man and his girlfriend with it. No sign of life had remained in the boiling water.

With those recent problems, on top of the usual challenges associated with running a National Park, Melanie Ward was doubly annoyed that the person sent to help her was, in her estimation, late. To be fair, the rep was supposed to begin work tomorrow. She had just *assumed* arrival tonight.

"God, I'd better get a decent night's sleep tonight. This is driving me crazy." She pushed her chair back from the monkey-pod desk and clicked off the work light. One last trip around to check things out before she took off for the day.

She left her office, refusing to look at the stack of incident reports. The car accident paperwork was uppermost in the stack, but the accidental death/suicide uppermost on her mind. She felt ill every time she thought of her rangers going right off the cliff after the man. A rush of adrenaline that quickly turned to nausea raced through her, and tears formed each time her imagination changed the scenario. Jody and T.J. were on leave now, and her heart went out to them as she thought of how they must feel. They claimed they'd be ready for the training, but she wasn't so sure. She missed their companionship and "best-friends" banter, not to mention their expertise as rangers.

She went to the dining room windows and felt herself relax, as she always did, as she viewed Puʻu Oʻo vent—300 feet deep, now dry and silent. At times it filled with molten lava, reminding all who watched that humanity was just a blip in the universe, and that Pele, Goddess of the Volcano, ruled this place.

Melanie—stocky, but in shape from years of hiking this rough terrain, and proud of her position and responsibility—had lost more sleep this past year than she cared to admit. Already working long hours, her load had increased, as incidents of violence in the park had also increased. None of her rangers had been seriously injured, but the patrons' abuse of drugs and alcohol in the park had gone up, and she felt an imperative to protect her staff, and help them protect themselves. She had drawn up statistics and paperwork to ask the national office for training funding. Then a memo had arrived, informing her that a training officer from the police department would come for a week to in-service her rangers and staff. Education in current drugs and weapons, physical defense, and changes in policies and procedures would be covered. Melanie was relieved that these steps would be taken, and was saddened that they were necessary.

She turned away from the window and checked the various rooms: the main dining room, the hotel rooms upstairs in the Victorian-style Volcano House, the gift shop. All was as it should be. She exited into the cooling night and crossed the drive to the cabins.

Natural geothermal vents allowed warm mist to escape, and she passed through clouds of wetness, warming her, then night air, chilling her on her way to the cabins. Occupied most of the year, the small cabins were cozy and private, with fireplaces, four-poster beds, and other homey touches.

After six P.M., in darkness, she crossed the second parking lot to check the Visitors' Center, museum and art gallery. Quiet here, too. Only security lights glowed. She inhaled and smelled the familiar volcano odor she loved, and the dampness of the vegetation.

She turned to head for her car and noticed lights on in the rehearsal hall. The play—what was it? *'Deathtrap?'*—opened in a couple of weeks, but according to the schedule the director had given her, there was no rehearsal tonight. Only the nightlights should be on.

Great. Now, what? Probably nothing, but she'd check it out. No point in getting Security out here for nothing, since she was already here.

How perfect, she thought. The way things were going at the park, why had she agreed to let them do 'Deathtrap'?

She crept up the wooden steps of the building to the lanai that completely surrounded the small, vintage structure. Boards creaked as she stepped to peer through a rear window. She could see nothing out of the ordinary. She tried the rear door. *Unlocked.* If someone had gotten in through a door left unlocked, she would kill that director guy. Better not be any damage, or she'd send him a bill.

Just as Melanie worked up a good head of steam, opened the door and stepped through, all the lights went out. She froze, listening. Then she heard the front door bang a millisecond later, and footsteps running away. She didn't move. Someone could still be inside. She didn't want to use her radio to call for help.

What if someone had heard her and realized she was there? *Better do something.* She listened until she was sure that no one was inside. The cold air blowing around her from the open back door helped her decide. She flipped the light switch, illuminating the room again. The burglar must have turned the lights off at the front switch as he went out. Or *she.*

"This won't look good," Melanie muttered, as she saw the portable white board set up, the papers, chairs and tables. She remembered a staff meeting with all the departments had taken place in this room today. *So much for blaming the flaky theatre people for leaving the building unlocked,* she thought.

Then she saw the note on the large center table, among the coffee cups and crumbs.

Dear Park and Madam Pele:
I'm sorry I took it. Please put it back for me so I won't have no more
bad luck.
Thank you. Peter Aronson
PS. The musim was closed and I didn't want to have this one more
day, so I left it here.

Holding down the note was a large *a'a* lava rock, jagged and beautiful. Next to it was a plastic baggie filled with "Pele's hair," the thin strings of windblown lava that dried into long, hair-like strands.

"They never learn." The Visitors' Center was full of this stuff. Melanie picked up the rock, note, and bag, and checked the rest of the room. She sure wasn't cleaning up after the department heads. She locked the back door, flipping on the outside light, then secured the front.

As she trudged back to her office to leave the lava, she laughed and mentally inventoried the notes and lava samples returned to the park over the years. This was one of the tamer ones, but typical. One guy had even mailed his shoes back from the Mainland, because he said the little lava rocks in the treads had given him a run of bad luck.

Madam Pele, Goddess of the Volcano, protected all that she deemed in her domain. All National Parks protected their flora and fauna, but Madam Pele was extra security against those who did manage to smuggle bits of lava home to the Mainland. Hundreds of packages arrived with letters of repentance and varying degrees of woe. She dropped off the samples and note, and relocked her office.

A rental car was just pulling into the spot next to hers. A thirty-ish red-headed *haole* got out and said, "You wouldn't be Melanie Ward, would you?"

"Yes, I am. How can I help you?" Melanie used her, *I'm here to serve the public, but hurry up because I'm off now* voice.

"I'm Officer Katrina Ogden, the training officer from Honolulu PD." The woman stuck out her hand.

Melanie shook it. "Nice to meet you. I'm off now, and really beat. It's been a helluva day."

"Can you tell me where I'm staying tonight, and maybe we can meet for breakfast?"

Melanie liked the woman's open face, green-blue eyes and fly-away hair. As the officer rummaged in her trunk, eventually pulling out a sweatshirt with the Magnum PI logo, Melanie assessed her.

Taller than herself by a couple of inches, and slimmer but strong-looking, Officer Ogden had a narrow face with a pointed nose, giving her an elfin appearance—far from menacing. But she also had an air of confidence and capability that made Melanie's burden feel just a little bit lighter.

With relief and a surge of new energy, Melanie led the way to the beautiful Volcano House dining room.

CHAPTER SIX

From Jerry's house, K.O. had driven directly to Hawai'i Volcanoes National Park in the gathering dusk. She had passed remembered landmarks, like the Solid Waste Transfer Station in Waiohinu, known locally as "da dump," nearly invisible on a hairpin curve. As she had coasted through the adorable town of Na'alehu, the intoxicating smell of the Punalu'u Hawaiian Sweet Bread factory had wafted into the car, and, as always, she coveted the old Victorian home that housed the local doctor.

Periodically, small signs stuck on sticks, or posted onto existing signs admonished the public with, "No Spray," and "No Poison", meaning that the highway department should not spray the shoulder for weed abatement.

Descending out of Na'alehu, she went by Whittington Beach Park, a beautiful coastal area with an actual beach—a rarity on this island that grew rapidly as fresh lava added to its acreage. Most of the Big Island's shoreline consisted of cliffs and large rocks, nearly inaccessible except by boat or long hike. Beautiful sands, ranging from gray to green to black, made Big Island beaches unique.

From Whittington, it was a straight shot for forty miles to the park entrance. As darkness fell, K.O. was forced to concentrate on her driving after her tiring but fulfilling day. About thirty miles from the park, she finally picked up a Hilo radio station to help her stay awake. Up 'til then, any signal had been blocked by rocks and curves, and listening to the engine's purr had been hypnotic.

At the entrance to the golf course and Volcano Winery, she made a mental note to return and buy her co-workers, Selena and Lana, some macadamia nut wine.

At nearly seven P.M., and pitch black, she finally pulled into the park and passed the empty tollbooth, wound past the Visitors' Center, museum and art gallery, and followed the arrows to the parking lot fronting Volcano House, the hotel and restaurant perched on the rim of the caldera. Then, as she switched off her headlights and engine, she saw a forty-ish woman in a park ranger uniform cross the parking lot from Volcano House, and head towards the car in the space next to her rental.

Ready to fall into bed, she said to herself, "This can't be the one person I need. That would be too good to be true," before getting out of the car and approaching Melanie Ward.

Ms. Ward looked exhausted, and her polite manner indicated to K.O. that she just wanted to get home. K.O. knew that feeling well, having dealt with the public in Records and Identification at the Honolulu Police Department for two years.

Thank God for my transfer, she thought for the fiftieth time, I probably would have gone certifiable and shot somebody if I had stayed in that department. *Not really,* she corrected herself, but some days . . .

To her surprise, after shaking hands, Ms. Ward seemed to change gears. "Tell you what. I really am dead, but I do need to talk to you before the first briefing, which so happens to be a breakfast meeting." She smiled. "So, why don't we have dinner here in Volcano House—the best food around really—and we can talk. How does that sound?"

"Great. I'm freezing, but it's gorgeous here. Just the way I remember it." K.O. pulled on a ratty sweatshirt she grabbed from her luggage.

"You've been here before?"

"Oh, yes. I love the Big Island; it's my favorite place, but the job, you know—O'ahu's it. I visit as often as I can. That's one reason I was so happy to get this assignment."

As they crossed the parking lot to Volcano House, K.O said, "I just realized, I'm starved. Is this too casual?" She gestured at her sweatshirt.

Melanie shook her head, as she led them to a corner table in the elegant dining room. K.O. felt a little underdressed, but, after all, Ms. Ward was still in the uniform that she'd obviously worn all day. The room was quite warm compared to outdoors, so K.O. removed her Magnum PI sweatshirt and decided that in her black slacks and green blouse, *sans* sweatshirt, she looked fine.

A busy waitress dropped off menus and two waters, shot a "Hey, Melanie, be right back; sorry, eh? All jam up!" and flew off to a large party near the window.

Everything on the menu looked good, and the smells wafting through the dining room made K.O.'s stomach growl again, even more loudly. She refused to look up, but heard Ms. Ward stifle a laugh.

K.O. quickly decided what to order and set down her menu. "I appreciate you seeing me this late, Ms. Ward. I know how tired you must be."

"No problem. And call me Melanie, please. You don't know the half of it. But I'd like to tell you some now and get a jump on the briefing tomorrow. I don't know how much time we'll have to get you up to speed, but we're having some problems in the park, and that's why you're here, Ms. Ogden. To train the rangers in hand-to-hand stuff, drugs, weapons . . ." Her voice trailed off, and her round face looked haggard.

"Call me K.O. I was informed this was a preventive measure, really, for your park. NPS informed me that Mainland parks were seeing an escalation in violence, and some of those parks are so remote and small-staffed, it just makes sense to increase the rangers' skills. But here?" She raised a questioning eyebrow.

"Maybe that was true in the past, but no more. We see all the same problems the Mainland parks have. Particularly lately. We've had several incidents recently that have set us all on edge. In fact, two of my rangers are on leave now for something that happened last week. You probably read about it in the paper," she added glumly.

"Okay, what can I get for you?" The waitress was back. A strand of gray hair stuck to the sweat on her cheek, and her pudgy body shook with each rapid breath.

"Izzy, take a breath. Have you had your break, yet? You look fried." Melanie looked concerned as she spoke to the older woman.

"No can. Jessie called in sick, las' minute, her boy t'rowing up again." She saw K.O. and said, "Oh, sorry, eh?"

"No problem," K.O. answered.

"Izzy, this is K.O., the HPD officer who's come to train everyone. She's here to help, so treat her good." Melanie patted the woman's wrinkled hand. "Don't worry. We're fine. Just take your time. Get rid of that large party and I'll see what I can do, okay?" She asked K.O., "Ready? Know what you want?" K.O. nodded and they both ordered. The frazzled waitress took off towards the kitchen.

"If it's not one thing, it's another. I'll be right back." Melanie headed to the kitchen and was gone for several minutes. When she returned, she collapsed in her chair, and smiled.

"Poor Izzy. Poor kitchen! It's a zoo back there. I called someone from housekeeping who used to wait tables. She'll be here in a few.

"Okay, back to the problem at hand. *My* problem." She laughed tiredly.

K.O. listened as Melanie outlined the growing troubles in the park, including last week's car accident and the more recent accident/suicide. The park's investigation team, meaning Melanie and her staff, hadn't decided how that would be classed. Hilo PD wasn't talking.

"I'm so glad you're here. I feel like it's all on me. It isn't really, but it feels like it. I was just compiling stats and requests for help from NPS when I got the memo that they were arranging a training session. I guess I had put off really documenting the need, because I thought they might find the fault was mine—say I should have prevented problems, instead of cleaning up after them." Melanie took a big slug of water, too late to hide the tears welling up.

K.O. also drank, giving Melanie a moment to recover.

"I'd like to review your incident reports. I'm not here as an investigator, but I can help you that way. Maybe we'll see a pattern, or I'll find places to tighten up security. Who knows?"

Melanie grinned. "That'd be great."

Their food arrived and they dug in. After they had eaten, pushed their plates away, and stared at the dessert menu a moment, they resumed their conversation.

Melanie chuckled. "I swear half my problem is I'm not eating right. This schedule and the stress play havoc on my diet. Woman cannot live on Twinkies alone."

K.O. laughed, too. "You're right about that. We need Diet Pepsi and wine to make it a balanced diet."

"Oh, I knew I was leaving something out."

A young woman in a dining room uniform approached their table with two dessert plates. "Here, these are from Izzy, on the house." She set down two scrumptious-looking slices of macadamia nut pie.

"Thanks, Bernice. And thanks for coming in at the last minute. We all appreciate it," Melanie said.

The woman nodded and smiled.

"Oh, God, I love this!" K.O. moaned, as she took a bite. "Let me guess, Kona chip?"

Bernice laughed. "Yup. You sure know your pie."

"This is Mac Pies, out of Keahou, right? It's my favorite—I'd know it anywhere!"

Bernice laughed again and left them.

K.O. finally pushed the plate away, after eating every crumb. "I made an outline of my plan for the week. I'd like to start with an overview and a day by day breakdown of the schedule. I understand I'm to plan on two sessions per subject to cover the different shifts and staffs?" Melanie nodded. "Will the staff just come to whichever session they can, or have they been assigned?"

"They've been assigned according to their duty rotation, but that may change if people call in sick, or God forbid, something happens, and we need everybody out there."

"Okay. I'll have them sign in at the various sessions, so I can track who's there and who's missing. I've built in the last day for make-ups for those who missed something. This training earns them a certification, but only if they complete it. I wanted to make sure we'd have time to make up any missed sessions. If they miss too much, I can't do anything about it, but I wanted to try."

"That's great, K.O. I appreciate your flexibility, and I'm so glad it was *you* they sent! Tomorrow comes early, so let me get you the reports; they're in my office."

Melanie signed the dinner check saying, "It's on me, I'm just glad you're here," then led K.O. towards her cozy office.

In the parking lot, she said, "Just follow me. I'll drive you around the crater to the barracks where you'll stay. I'll say sorry in advance. It's not the Royal Hawaiian, that's for sure."

"That's fine. I figured it would be something of the sort." K.O. drove, following Melanie's car to the U.S. Army part of the park.

Definitely not for the tourists, K.O. decided, as Melanie pulled up next to the corrugated-metal quonset huts. "And definitely not Volcano House," she said, as she tugged her bag out of the trunk and followed Melanie inside.

CHAPTER SEVEN

"What the hell happened?" Rudy demanded. Gerald and Jolene sat opposite Rudy, a vast expanse of koa desk between them. Rudy's office, in his opulent house outside Volcano, Hawaii, bespoke extreme wealth. Hand woven carpets, antique vases, original art, were the trappings of the luxurious estate. Security monitors, dogs, and electric fencing enclosed five of his twenty acres. No one got in or out undetected. Lush landscaping hid the house from view off Highway 11.

Jolene sat, smug and mute, in the kapa cloth chair.

"Well?" Rudy said. "Somebody better say something. Tommy's dead, and one of our best growing sites eliminated. For what?"

Gerald shifted in his chair. "Jolene said Tommy was getting difficult, and was uh, skimming."

"Is that true, J?"

"Sure, Rudy, you know I take care of you. You family." Jolene sat, composed and smiling, as Rudy studied her. She met his gaze. His handsome features, marred by acne scars from adolescence, gave no indication of his thoughts. He swept a hand through his curly brown hair and stood.

"I don't like this. I'm out a good guy, and a good spot. I'm going to be watching you two."

Gerald swallowed nervously, looking up at Rudy. "I just follow orders, you know, Rudy. She killed him. I didn't even know he was cheating you." The words sounded weak, even to Gerald.

"Cheating or not, dead is dead. Neither of you should think you are immune to that. You're not the only people who work for me. Do good, and I'll see you're taken care of. Screw up again, and the only way you leave is in pieces."

Jolene seemed unmoved by the threat. "Yeah, Rudy, okay. I got a good crop in the tube now, and Gerald, he know his stuff. We changed the nitrogen and the light exposure. They doin' real good now. The first crop is upside down now, drying. We gotta do something about the water though. It's a pain in da ass to haul. We gotta rig some catchment thing, with underground pipes, 'cause these plants, dey suckin' up so much water . . . Can get someone to do that, Rudy?"

"No, you take care of it. This part of the project was supposed to be just the three of you. Now it's down to two, but that's your problem. You know I keep my growing and harvesting crews and locations separate. I'm keeping it that way." He looked at Gerald. "Take care of it, Gerald, yeah?"

"Yeah, Rudy. I take care of it."

"Are we *pau,* already?" Jolene asked.

"Yes, we're done." Rudy stalked out of his office as if Gerald and Jolene no longer existed. Gerald shot a bewildered glance at Jolene. She ignored him, picked up her purse, and went out to the truck.

"Come on, Gerald!" she screeched from the cab. Gerald sighed and followed her out.

Gerald drove the beat-up truck out of the grounds and turned onto the highway, towards the little town of Volcano. A light rain began to fall, and Gerald flicked on the wipers. The headlights weakly picked out the road ahead, and the nearly rubberless blades scraped in protest across the cracked windshield.

In silence, Gerald pulled up in front of Jolene's coffee shack. He stared straight ahead, engine running, lights and wipers on.

"Gerald," Jolene said softly, "you like come in, or what?"

"No."

"Come on, Gerald. It's raining. You know what the rain does to me. Forget Rudy and the crop. We work together now, jus' us." Her nails stroked his forearm lightly, raising goose bumps among the dark hairs.

"Just get out, Jolene. I'm tired. I want to go home." Gerald still stared straight ahead.

"Gerald, we could be good together. No one in our way, now."

No response.

"Gerald, you goin' be sorry. I'm not a good enemy." Jolene slammed the door of the truck and ran to the house.

Gerald didn't wait. He yanked the truck into gear, and gravel spun as he raced away from Jolene.

He didn't notice her purse on the floor as it slid under the front passenger seat.

CHAPTER EIGHT

K.O. took stock of her lodgings. *Just like the military movies,* she mused. A long, narrow room, edged with metal bunk beds on a cement floor. Exposed two-by-fours and four-by-fours, connected by rusted, corrugated metal.

A bathroom with four toilet stalls, four slimy-looking showers and one cracked mirror sat at the opposite end. The far door led to a connecting barracks, and another door led outside.

Although tired, K.O. could not sleep. The plastic-covered mattress rustled every time she moved, and she was sure the additional rustlings were rodent in origin. She lay on a bottom bunk near the door, eyeing the vast expanse of metallic shadows stretching before her. Curtainless windows let in shafts of moonlight that dimmed and brightened as clouds obscured them. A rumbling noise gradually increased to a pounding she recognized as rain on the roof. Water cascaded down the troughs and crashed outside the thin metal barrier next to her head.

She felt alone, and lonely. A whole week by herself in this cavern? Maybe she should ask to be moved to a smaller space, at least. This huge barracks was creepy.

Her thoughts drifted to Alani. In the course of her previous case, she had reconnected with her friend Lana's brother, finding that their initial attraction to each other years ago still burned strong. A tickling in her stomach hinted that she might like to pursue *any* kind of relationship with him. She hoped he would visit her during this trip, as he had suggested he might.

Because of the injuries she had sustained on her last case, as well as her expertise in field training, intervention and crime prevention, K.O. had been offered this cake-walk interim assignment: training sessions at the park. She was to sit in a room full of sedentary administrators, staff, and NPS rangers, and update them on the latest techniques, weapons and drugs. A few slides, a few samples, lectures, and some Physical Training. Practically a vacation.

The rain slackened to a gentle whooshing sound that K.O. found soothing, and she finally drifted off.

Strange noises, feet running, thumps and laughter pulled her, much too early, from sleep. From her corner bunk, K.O. saw the door burst open, and the room was invaded. Hundreds, maybe thousands of teenagers swept into the barracks, boys and girls, filling the space from top to bottom with luggage, slippers, jackets, coolers, and noise.

K.O. cowered in her bunk and pulled the thin covers up high. She had gone to sleep in her underwear. Her bags sat on the upper bunk, just a few feet above her, but it might as well have been a mile.

"Please, let this be a nightmare," she prayed, as a teenaged girl threw herself on the bunk opposite K.O., flipped her slippers under it, and cranked up a boom box. Her one exposed eye was suddenly covered by a "Kona Gold" sweatshirt the girl threw onto K.O.'s bunk.

That was enough.

"Hey!" K.O. shouted. The boom box volume decreased minutely. "Hey, you!" K.O. called again. The sweatshirt was removed, and K.O. freed her arms from the covers. "What's going on?"

"Sorry, eh?" The girl indicated the sweatshirt. "Camp!" she called exuberantly.

This was worse than being alone in the barracks. She revised her count, and decided the invasion numbered only about fifty teenagers, all shapes, ages and sizes, unpacking, laughing, throwing things. No sign of an adult. What the hell kind of camp was this?

She was about to inquire, when five adults entered quickly, two of them supporting a girl.

"Kimmy, move, yeah?" one of the women called. They placed the sweating, disoriented girl on Kimmy's bunk, across from K.O.

"Somebody get me a kit!"

"I got one here, Jane." A small machine was passed to the woman squatting at the girl's side.

"Thanks, Sharon," Jane said. Sharon rummaged in her fanny pack, and brought out what looked like ketchup packets.

"I've got glucose here, too," Sharon said. The activity at the far end of the room continued, but near Kimmy's bunk, a circle of sober-looking teens gathered.

K.O. watched as Jane poked the girl's slack finger, drawing a drop of blood. She put it on a small strip, and inserted it into a calculator-sized gizmo.

"Sharon, get Dr. Doug and the rest of the meds. The cooler is in my pile. Get Nancy to start the rest testing their blood sugars. We're running late, and they're going to start crashing unless we get some food into them." Jane indicated the kids with a sweep of her hand. Sharon nodded and dashed out.

All eyes focused on the drama across from K.O. She sat up and carefully groped the bunk above, then brought her bag down. She found a T-shirt and sweats and slid them on, under the covers. She sat up, feet dangling, and watched intently.

Jane's meter beeped. "Oh, my God. Over 900. Doug! Insulin!"

A man appeared with an I.V. drip, and deftly inserted the needle.

Nancy shooed kids back to their bunks and piles of junk, where they poked their own fingers and began what was obviously a practiced ritual of measuring out medicine from vials into syringes and injecting themselves. The noise level dropped to almost nil. In the silence, K.O. heard the labored breathing of the nearly comatose girl in Kimmy's bunk, the click of fingers flicking bubbles out of syringes, and the slaps, pats and gasps as kids injected themselves with varying degrees of skill and pain. A few kids called for help or advice. Should I take my shot now? I feel low. Can I have a snack? The adults, if not all medical personnel, seemed knowledgeable in their care, and moved through the group, monitoring and assisting.

Jane, with Dr. Doug, still squatted near the red-faced girl.

"Come on, Angela, honey. You'll feel better soon," Jane said. She turned to Dr. Doug. "I'll stay. You get the rest of the kids to the dining hall. When's Gomez coming?"

"I'm not sure. This morning sometime. He had early hospital rounds at Tripler, then he was going to hop the next flight and drive out. Depends how the rounds went, I guess."

"Okay, thanks. I'll call you if anything happens. I'm going to check her every fifteen minutes until her sugar drops."

"If it doesn't come down sufficiently in four hours, I'll check her into Hilo Hospital."

"Okay. It'd be such a shame for her to come all the way from Molokai for Diabetes Camp, and then miss it like this." Jane patted Angela's hand, then held it.

Dr. Doug and the other adults herded their charges out the far door. *Merciful silence.* Jane didn't seemed to notice K.O.

"Uh, hi. Excuse me?" K.O. spoke softly.

"Oh. Hi. Are you a camp volunteer?"

"No. I'm here to help in the park. They put me in the barracks. How is she?"

"I'm not sure. She's always been a brittle one."

"Brittle?"

"Yes. Blood sugars that are hard to control—up one minute, then down the next."

"Are you her mom?"

"No, I'm a nurse at Queen's Hospital, and a volunteer with the American Diabetes Association Youth Camp. Angel's been coming to our camp since she was four. She lives on Molokai, and her control's not so good. Usually our camp's on O'ahu, but this year we're having it here on the Big Island."

"I'm from O'ahu, too. Where is your camp?"

"Mokuleia. Camp Erdman, the YMCA camp?"

"Oh, yeah. I know it."

Angela moaned, and her eyelids fluttered.

"Come on, Angel. You"ll be fine. Jane's here. All the kids are having breakfast now. Let's get you back on your feet. You don't want to miss out on all the fun, do you?" Jane glanced at K.O. "So, what are you doing here?"

"I'm doing some training sessions for the park service this week. How long are you folks here?"

Jane laughed. "All week. Don't worry. They're good kids. Noisy, exuberant, but good. We'll try not to bother you. Maybe you can join us at the fire ring sometime?'" At K.O.'s expression, Jane laughed again. "Well, maybe not, but you're welcome to."

Jane pulled out the little meter, and poked Angela's finger again. "Good girl," she said, with obvious relief. "She's responding to the insulin. Down to 700."

"Is that high?"

"Oh, my yes. Normal blood sugar usually runs 125-150 after a meal, and fasting, first thing in the morning, lower. We try our best to control it at camp, and teach them about balance in diet and exercise, but when they go home, back to their friends and families, it all goes out the window."

"So, 900 is really high?"

"Yes, that's quite dangerous. We have everything that the hospital would, though, so unless they don't respond or get worse, we try to keep the kids at camp. We've got fluids in her, too. Sugar that high means ketones, dehydration—complications, if not monitored."

"What are ketones?"

"Toxins. Poison the system. When the sugar's too high, the body can't process it and kicks ketones into the urine. Angel here will be on bed rest until she's stable. She's a pistol, though, and she'll be up and around by dinner, just wait and see."

K.O. glanced at her watch and saw she had fifteen minutes to dress and get to the breakfast briefing.

"It was great to meet you, Jane. You too, Angela. I'd like to learn more about this. And your kids, too. I've got a meeting to rush to, but have a good day. Feel free to use my bunk if you need it. I can move anywhere. Whatever's good for you." She dragged her bag towards the bathroom. "Anything I can get for you?"

"No, thanks. Nice meeting you, too. I'm sure you'll see us around." Jane's attention went back to her charge, and K.O. hurried through her morning routine and flew out the door to her car.

CHAPTER NINE

K.O. raced into Melanie's office in Volcano House, but found it empty. She realized she had no idea where the briefing was to be held. *Breakfast meeting—maybe the dining room?* Detective Ogden, on the case.

She paused in the doorway, but didn't hear anything. *Shoots!* she thought. *I'm going to be late the first day. Way to set an example.*

A sudden burst of laughter from behind a partial wall guided her to a section of the dining room she hadn't noticed the night before.

A large group of rowdy NPS employees filled up several far tables, but K.O. was too distracted by the incredible view to give them more than a cursory glance. The far wall, from the waist up, was entirely windows. The gray-black crater that was Hale Mau Mau gaped below her. Volcano House sat literally on the edge of the crater.

Only a few feet and a lava wall between safety and a major sacrifice to Pele, Goddess of the Volcano. Not far enough from the edge. By a long shot. K.O., not happy with heights to begin with, found this view particularly alarming because of the foolish idea that one could just *step out* and soar, hundreds of feet above the crater floor, and thousands of feet across to the barren far side.

She felt a light touch at her elbow, and pulled herself away from the hypnotic vista. Like a sparrow to a cobra, she thought. She turned and saw Melanie at her side, and let herself be led to the waiting table.

In the silence that greeted her, she wondered how long she'd stood mesmerized by the view.

"Everyone, this is Katrina Ogden, from the Honolulu Police Department. She's here at the behest of the National Park Service to give us a week of training. She'll meet you all individually, I'm sure, but let's make her feel welcome."

Some half-hearted applause. *Maybe they just need some coffee. God knows I do,* K.O. thought.

Melanie pulled out a chair and poured a cup of coffee, gently pushing K.O. into the seat.

"I know it's early," Melanie continued, "and thank you for being here. I'll bring us all up to speed first on our needs here at the park, and why HPD and the NPS are working together. Breakfast will be out shortly, and it's family style. We'll just have big platters of stuff, and you help yourselves, all right?" She smiled and got a few answering grins.

Sounded good to K.O. She was starved. All that talk about blood sugars—highs, lows, crashing—made her thrilled she didn't have to go through that every day, but it had an odd effect on her appetite. She held herself back from snatching the whole fruit bowl when it was placed in front of her, making a mental note to ask Melanie about the campers later.

Melanie continued. "The first thing is the schedule, because if you are not on the same shifts all week, you may have to adjust accordingly. It's up to you to get in all your sessions and hours. K.O. will have you sign in, and if you miss something, she's graciously offered to have make-ups at the end of the week. We're all really trying to see you get your certification. Not only does that mean a pay bump, although a tiny one"—some laughter greeted this—"but it also updates your eligibility for employment at any other National Park." She passed out neatly organized packets, topped by the schedule on hot pink paper.

K.O. noted that the trainings would be held at several locations around the park. The only one she was familiar with was Volcano House. *Oh, yes,* she could probably find the Visitors' Center, too. She thought she had passed it coming in last night. A rec center of some kind sat in front of her barracks, and several sessions were in a building attached to it. K.O. bet those teenagers would find the rec center within minutes. Maybe she could get some help from them if she got too lost. One session was at an outdoor location "TBA."

"What's this one?" K.O. pointed to "TBA" and the notation of "Field Intervention and Defusing. *God, I hope they don't expect me to fool around with bombs,* K.O. thought, with a tiny bubble of panic. Her initial sense was that she was not quite welcomed at this party, except by Melanie, and she didn't know why.

"Don't worry," said Melanie, with a laugh. "It means, To Be Announced. We're wondering where the best place is for that one. Maybe you can help us decide later in the week."

"By 'best place', she means most dangerous," said a local-looking young man in uniform.

Melanie laughed. "Right, T.J. Any place you have in mind?"

"Yeah, how 'bout the fresh flow?" T.J. answered, smiling.

"Man, Teej." The extremely fair-skinned ranger next to T.J. groaned. Older than T.J. and also in uniform, the man smacked T.J. lightly on the head. "You didn't get enough befo'?" His attempt at a pidgin accent was laughable, and the employees did laugh at him, but in a teasing, gentle way that told K.O. this *haole* was a favorite, and also, that they thought his pidgin would never improve.

Nothing like a *haole* speaking bad pidgin to grate on the ear. K.O.'s run-ins with tourists speaking "guidebook" pidgin made her cringe, even thinking about them years later. Of course, it was great fodder for jokes at work, as she was sure this man's attempts were.

"Okay, Jody." T.J. shot a bit of roll into his friend's sandy hair.

"Am I going to have to separate you two?" Melanie asked, hands on hips. The group erupted into laughter. The tension was broken, and everyone dug into the food, orange juice, and Kona coffee with gusto.

K.O. poked Melanie. "What's 'Field Intervention and Defusing?'" K.O. had planned only some of the sessions; others had been handed down from the NPS level.

"When someone gets too rowdy, has too much to drink, for example. Instead of escalating it by your authority and uniform, you defuse the situation. Maybe save somebody from getting arrested. People do funny things when they're scared or nervous, you know."

K.O. did know. She was skilled at controlling a situation, calming people, soothing frayed nerves. Part of it was training, and part of it, despite her claims otherwise, was her personality. Make no mistake, she'd get into a scuffle in a minute, no hanging back, but her first choice was to avoid it. During her years in patrol, this trait had served her well. Since she'd been in Records and Identification, the need to pacify the general public while they moped around her office had worn thin, but she had certainly experienced more dangerous situations in her career.

She remembered a call to a bar fight at Diamond Lil's by the Honolulu airport—a biker hang-out, a place she sometimes went on her off-hours. She loved to play pool, the bands were usually good, and the dance floor was comparatively large. Because O'ahu was an island, and not that big, the biker population didn't change much, unlike the Mainland where hopping on a Harley and driving 500 miles could put one in another state. Consequently, K.O. knew most of the bikers, not only from work, but socially, too. Good to have friends from all walks of life, she had found.

On that occasion, K.O. knew other white cars—patrol cars—
would show up soon, and she was completely familiar with the
layout, so she entered the bar's back door. The band, a large group
with a horn section, played loudly, while military guys danced
with diminutive Asian partners. Between the restrooms and the
bar, a dozen pool tables looked like small green islands in a dark
sea.

K.O. surveyed the room. The conflict seemed isolated and
relatively unexciting, except for the man with blood gushing from
his face and dripping onto his shirt. A circle of onlookers watched
warily as an extremely large, balding *haole*, shirtless, in a black
leather vest faced him, loosely holding a knife.

"Hey, Tiny, it's K.O. What chu doin' brah?' K.O. asked him
gently.

The man turned slightly to see K.O., but kept the other man
in view. "Hey, K.O., this asshole tried to jump me." Nods of
agreement. No one seemed to be on the other man's side.

"Tiny, you know I gotta have the knife, yeah? Let's talk about
it. I don't want to take you in, 'less you make trouble. You gonna
make trouble?" K.O. waited and watched not only the two men,
but the crowd, as well. She raised her voice. "Unless you saw
something, you guys go back to what you were doing, yeah? It's
under control now." Since no one had seen a thing, despite it
happening at the next pool table, the crowd dispersed. She had
turned back to Tiny. "Tiny, I gotta figure this out before back up
shows up, you know that."

"Yeah, K.O." Tiny still clenched and unclenched his hand on
the knife, his eyes flicking back and forth from K.O. to the man.
His beefy body was rigid with anger, and K.O. knew he was making
a decision. It was entirely possible for Tiny to attack the man again,
for whatever reason, and disregard any consequences such as jail
time, damages, injury, or even death. K.O. wasn't sure whose death,
but knew Tiny was willing and able.

The other man seemed frozen, or in shock, blood still running freely. K.O. thought Tiny hadn't used the knife—maybe had just hit him.

"Tiny, don't make it worse. Give me the knife, brah."

Tiny handed her the knife, handle first. K.O. felt the tension leave her body. Adrenalin she didn't know had flowed made her wobbly. K.O.'s 5'7", 125-pound frame versus an enraged 6'4", 300-pound biker would not have made a pretty or lengthy physical confrontation.

Tiny sat on the end of a pool table, arms folded. K.O. noted that the young people playing on the table said not a word, but moved to the bar. She turned her attention to the other man.

"What's your name? Are you all right?" He was obviously not all right, but K.O. couldn't tell the extent of his injuries. Without warning, the man collapsed. K.O. rushed to his side and felt for a pulse. Weak, but there. Blood loss? Not that much.

K.O. yanked out her radio and tersely asked for help and an ambulance, then checked his respiration. He breathed. His heart beat, but he was pale and waxy. K.O. glanced at Tiny. He still sat, detached, arms folded on the pool table.

The man beneath her suddenly lunged and wrapped his hands around her throat in an incredible grip. The bar sounds faded as K.O. fought to breathe and to break his grasp. Her position blocked most spectators from seeing her peril between the game tables. If she rolled, he could get on top and have even more leverage and strength, if that were possible. With both hands on her neck, at least he wasn't going for her gun. But someone else in the bar might. Where the hell was back up? She punched him in the throat. Nothing. She kneed his groin. No reaction. K.O. knew then that he was flying, maybe PCP. Superhuman strength and behavior swings. *Great.*

Then Tiny was there, wrestling with the man whose grip did not slacken. As she felt herself giving in to the lack of oxygen, the space seemed full of uniforms. She found out later that it took five people, not including herself, to drag the man away from her.

Later, in booking, he'd been put in a straight jacket and had broken out of it, another wrestling match ensuing in the holding cell.

Since then, Tiny had never given her, or any other officer that she knew of, any trouble. Sending him a thank you note hadn't hurt either, she suspected. She doubted he'd become a model citizen, but she'd written up a favorable report, charges hadn't been filed, and the blood stains at Diamond Lil's had become just another story.

* * *

As K.O. ate, she glanced around the tables, and decided that this could not be all the employees at the park. She saw a number of uniformed rangers, but the others she assumed to be clerical or administrative. An air of camaraderie enveloped the group, and K.O. listened to bits of conversation, work-related questions, and old jokes.

Melanie sat to her left. To her right, a round-faced, sour-looking man in a rumpled, cigarette-smelling, blue suit shoveled in his food and conversed with no one.

As she took in his appearance, he suddenly caught her eye, and aimed his yolky fork at her. "What are you doing here?"

Caught off guard by his aggression, K.O. stammered. "I, uh, am here to train the staff."

"No. I mean *you.*" He shook his fork, spattering his blue jacket with yellow. "Why are *you* here?"

"I'm not sure what you mean. A chain of memos, I guess, from the NPS to the department. I was asked to take this assignment." K.O. was not about to divulge that she thought her particular appointment was, in part, occupational therapy. True, she was a Field Training Officer, skilled and knowledgeable in the area; she had been on the leading edge of the department's computer development, and had further educated herself by voluntary special trainings offered by other agencies including the FBI and ATF.

She was not the only officer to accomplish this. She was, however, the only officer with such a background that HPD wanted to relocate for a bit, and since they had to pay her anyway, they might as well have the National Park Service do it for them. That was K.O.'s reasoning, however, not anything she'd been told.

The man seemed dissatisfied with her answer, but hunched over his plate again. K.O. gratefully turned her attention back to the table and caught the end of what she thought must have been a dirty joke, probably at Jody's expense, given his hibiscus-red face and nervous laughter.

She felt a poke from her suave tablemate to the right. It had better not be with that nasty fork, she thought, or I'm gonna take that fork and ram it—"Yes?" she asked politely, turning to face him.

"Okay. How come Hilo PD was left totally out of it?"

K.O. started to get the picture. "Out of the training, you mean?"

"Yeah." He looked at her expectantly, eyes narrowing in his fleshy face. Oily sweat gave his face a shiny reflective surface. K.O. decided it came from eating so fast and so much. Hard work, that.

"I don't really know. Maybe no one at Hilo was available now?" He shook his head. "Or, maybe whatever the NPS wanted, no one in Hilo had the training?"

He shook his head again. "My brother is the best cop in Hilo, and he's a black belt. You tell me why he didn't get this gig? Some girly from outer island and a fuckin' *haole*, too." He pushed back from the table, threw his napkin on top of his eggy plate, and walked out muttering, "I gotta get some air."

"What is his problem?" K.O. asked Melanie, who, like the others at the table, didn't seem the slightest bit disturbed at his exit.

"Oh, that's Clayton Hsu. His brother's in Hilo PD, and a real screw-up. He's barely holding on in the department, he has so many complaints against him, but Clayton won't hear a bad word about him. It doesn't help that Clayton's a chain smoker, and the NPS says he has to quit, or his health insurance won't cover any related health problems. He has to go on a 'program', so he can keep his medical insurance. He's got a death wish, though. He still smokes, like a pack a day, wears a patch, and chews that nicotine gum. I swear to God, the guy's mental."

K.O. was about to ask why the NPS kept him at all, when Melanie stood, banged a spoon on her juice glass, and said, "Okay, I'm going to turn this over to K.O. now, your boss and trainer for the week," and sat down, looking expectantly at K.O.

CHAPTER TEN

K.O. stood uncertainly and pasted on a smile. "Hi, everyone. Good breakfast." A few chuckles—a good sign. "As Melanie said, I'm here for a week to give you the certification training in defense for the NPS. The program is according to guidelines developed way above me, so if you don't like it, it's not my fault." A few more laughs. "I'll try to make this as painless as possible, both literally and figuratively, so why don't we just get to the schedule and workshop contents?" K.O. riffled through her pages. "Please take out the orange background and objective sheets." She whispered to Melanie, "Thank you for color-coding everything. You're a lifesaver!"

"Sure thing." Melanie smiled.

"Okay. If you'll review the statistics on violence in NPS parks, you'll see an increase over the last ten years, with a big jump in the last two. This particular jump is what has the park service concerned. Mainland parks can be extremely large and remote" —there was some rumbling from her audience—"and I'm sure you all know better than I the area and staff per square mile in these parks. Compared to some parks, Volcanoes isn't the biggest. Nor is it as difficult to patrol as the mostly underwater parks!"

This time there was a genuine laugh. "So, to combat this rise, NPS is increasing security and training in all the parks. Since Hawai'i is remote, I was recruited because I have the background, rather than having NPS send over another staff member who might serve better in the Mainland."

She hoped that would offset any further hostility at her presence. She sipped her water. Clayton Hsu returned from his fresh air— smoking break, more like. K.O. wrinkled her nose as pungent cigarette fumes drifted off Clayton.

"Okay. On the next orange page is the list of actual crimes, not only here, but in the Mainland. HVP is in boldface, in the middle of the grouping. Not too much crime, or too many incidents, but you can see it's increased here, as well. The third orange page tells how NPS and I will prepare you for this and upgrade your training. Specifically, the objectives we need to meet and the number of hours and particular training you'll need. Questions, so far?"

"What if we don't want to do this?" Clayton Hsu asked.

"Fair question. But not really mine to answer. I am just here to train you. If you don't want to do it, you need to take that up with your supervisor and/or the National Park Service. I do know that you won't receive your certification or the pay increase without completing the hours. The only flexibility I have is what I already said I'd do. That is, to provide a reasonable amount of make-up time for those who have extenuating circumstances. Some we can't make up. You either make your session, or you lose out."

"Which ones can't be made up?" a woman dressed in office-clothes asked.

"What's your name?"

"Miranda Sales."

"Well, Miranda, we can't make up the 'out in the field' sessions like Contacts and Confrontations, Drug and Weapon Assessment and Removal. Those particular classes have one mandatory session, because they'll take most of the day, and also include an ordnance segment. You'll be roughing it, dealing with situations you can't control. We will only do it once. Good. Anything else?

When no one raised another question, K.O. continued, "Going to the green sheets—this is your list of classes, and under each class, it lists materials and dress code. Indoor weaponless defense, you can wear whatever, but see that outdoor class? You need hiking apparel and your kits you'd have as rangers, etc. I know some of you aren't out in the field, but you never know when this could come knocking on your office door. You have to be prepared, and pray you never need it." She looked at each person in turn, even Clayton, and detected a glint of respect and attention.

After a moment, she continued. "So, we'll break while you get dressed, undressed"—more laughter—"organized and supplied. I see our first session is at 1 P.M. in the military rest camp conference room. See you there. Bring your questions!"

There was shuffling and discussion as people left, and K.O. packed up her materials.

"So, want a tour?" Melanie asked. "We have a couple hours. I have a picnic lunch on standby in the kitchen. We can do the upper park, take a short hike. Or do you need time to prepare for the session?"

K.O. looked at her afternoon session. She was glad she'd decided to start easy. Drugs and weapons. She'd packed some samples and some look-alikes, and had thought to begin by getting to know everyone and generating discussion and feedback. She was ready.

"Nope. I'm ready for today's session, and it'd be helpful to get to know the ins and outs of the park. I've been here before, but it's been a long time, and I'm sure there are places I need to see that are off the normal tourist track."

"You're right, there. So, what do you need to do? We'll start out around here, the buildings and offices, and then come back and get our lunch. We'll need to drive the crater rim and have our picnic, then a short hike, and back here for the session—sound good?"

It sounded better than good to K.O. Fresh air, a change of

scenery, the magic and mana of the spirit of the volcano—just what she needed. "Great. Let me put my stuff in the car before we go. And hit the bathroom!"

Melanie laughed. "I'd better do that, too. Don't want to have to write myself a ticket for criminal littering!" K.O. laughed, too, at the reference to public peeing.

A few minutes later they met outside Melanie's office, and she quickly walked them through both gift shops, the kitchen, and the rest of the hotel, introducing staff as they went.

They left Volcano House and crossed the parking lot to the Visitors' Center, museum, and art gallery. K.O. was fascinated by the samples of lava mailed back to the park, and the accompanying letters with tales of woe attributed to Madam Pele's wrath at the theft of her property—that is, anything in the park. She not only guarded her lava, but also the sacred 'ohelo berries, said to be her favorite. Dangerous to pick on the way to the volcano—however, once there, if the first berries were sacrificed to her, it was said to be safe to pick and eat all one liked on the return trip.

K.O. could have stayed for hours in the Visitors' Center, but after brief introductions, they walked to the art gallery next door. Here, she couldn't resist buying four lava coasters, each engraved with a petroglyph. She chose two canoe paddlers and two spear-laden warriors, charmed by their primitive stick-like figures. She saw other items she knew she'd have to return for later.

"Are you sure the lava coasters are okay to take?" she asked Melanie, only half-joking.

"Yup. Blessed and everything. Okay, here is the building where most of our conferences and larger meetings are held." Melanie pulled open the door and flipped on the light. K.O. saw a large, nearly empty room with a stage at one end.

"Is this where the plays are performed?" she asked.

"Yes. Something is being practiced in here most nights, now. The show starts next week sometime. Too bad you won't be here to see it."

"Oh, I know! I might stay for it, though. My friend Jerry is the director. They're doing 'Deathtrap.' He said I could come to the dress rehearsal if I wasn't here for opening. I'll have to see. But I'm definitely going to see the show. Jerry and I go way back." K.O. had walked to the stage and was peeking behind the closed curtain.

"So, this is it," Melanie said. "We should get going. Gotta pick up the lunch and do the crater rim."

"Okay, sure." K.O. let the curtain drop, filled with fond memories of performing past roles in community theater productions. Something about a stage, any stage, she thought. Ask her to give a speech, and she felt distinctly uncomfortable. She could do it, of course, as part of the job, but ask her to *become* someone else—that was heaven.

The women returned to the Volcano House dining room. "Hang on a sec while I get the picnic," Melanie told K.O.

"Okay, I'll be outside, taking in the view." K.O. indicated the small viewing area outside the back door. Melanie nodded and disappeared into the kitchen. K.O. went out into a brisk and unexpected breeze blowing off the crater. She stood on the low wall with the other tourists and looked down into the pit. She imagined it filled with fire, molten lava popping and bubbling up the sides. Directly below her, scrub brush tumbled away towards the bottom, but the other side of the crater, far into the park, was a moonscape. Flat, gray expanses of lava, broken only by park buildings and mountains of crumbly-looking but solid boulders. Even the sky was gray today, the pewter horizon blending with the earth. A white-gray cloud of steam rose in the distance, a huge plume even from this far away, where molten lava rushed into the sea, adding acres of land to the island. The air smelled heavy and wet, and K.O. wondered if it might rain, or if that was just the smell of the volcano.

K.O. felt invaded by a power larger than herself as she looked over the barren landscape. In her mind, she saw a single-file line of cloth-wrapped Hawaiians, crossing barefoot over the lava on the far rim to the edge of the precipice. The first in line was a large woman, whose copper skin glowed in the strange light. She carried a wooden bowl gently, reverently before her. Her unbound hair streamed down her back, held in place by a crown of leaves. The *kahuna*—the priest.

Several people behind her were similarly dressed, but carried drums, cloth bags and woven mats. A man in a short loincloth carried a *kahili*—a yellow-feathered staff that stretched high above him. More women followed, clad in ti leaf skirts of green and brown, leaf anklets and bracelets, bright spots of color in the bleakness. Several carried staffs, but none so regal as the yellow feathers. They moved in complete silence, but for the soft padding of their feet, as they made their way and finally knelt at the edge. The *kahuna* raised her arms high, and opened her mouth in chant, her *mele* rising and falling. The man's *malo* flapped in the breeze, and K.O. wondered what he had on underneath. This irreverent thought brought her out of her daze, and she blinked. The far rim was empty of dancers, *malo*-clad or otherwise.

"Ready?" Melanie asked. "Picnic aboard." She held out a stuffed backpack.

"Yes," K.O. answered, her gaze returning to the crater. "Do you guys ever have like, ceremonies here?"

"What do you mean? The rooms get rented for meetings and stuff. Like that?"

"No. I mean, like native Hawaiian stuff?"

"Oh, sure. This is sacred ground you know. Nothing's going on right now, though. Ready?" She marched back through the hotel to the parking lot. She unlocked her car saying, "You're gonna love this. Our first stop will really whet your appetite!" As K.O. fastened her seatbelt, Melanie chuckled mysteriously, then took off with tires squealing.

CHAPTER ELEVEN

Melanie drove through lush foliage into a dryer forested area. She swung the small car off the main road into a parking lot nearly ringed by steaming pools.

"Oh, my God. What is that horrible smell?" K.O. gasped.

"A good day at the sulphur pits!" Melanie said. "Hope you like egg salad, 'cause that's what the kitchen packed for lunch!"

"No way." K.O. released her seatbelt and exited. The smell wasn't so bad upwind.

The women wandered along the path among the pits and read the various signs.

"It always gives me the creeps to think that what I'm seeing is only a fraction of what's going on underground," K.O. said.

"Yeah, I know what you mean. The scientists have surveyed the park and all the trails are safe, but still . . ." They headed back to the car. "You wouldn't believe how many tourists think they know better than we do what is safe out here. I mean, the closest most of them have been to an active volcano is their kid's science project."

Melanie continued driving on the road circling the large crater of Hale Mau Mau. "This should look familiar," she said, as she pulled into the military area containing K.O.'s barracks.

"Yeah. It's not too bad, though."

Melanie parked in front of a lava-faced building, reminiscent of Mainland field-stone edifices. "I'll take you in and show you around, so you'll know where your meeting rooms are. It'd look bad for the instructor to get lost." She smiled and held the door for K.O.

Inside, the lobby area was dark, cool and quiet. A large fireplace filled one wall, and comfortable-looking overstuffed furniture dotted the room, inviting weary travelers to rest and converse.

At the desk a woman glanced up from her paperwork and smiled. "Howzit, Boss? Checkin' up?" She chuckled, and K.O. decided 'the boss' was well-liked, from the evidence she'd seen so far.

"Suze, this is K.O., the training officer. She'll be here a week, and is staying in the barracks."

"Hi."

"Hi." They shook hands. "Oh, I'm staying with the camp kids, and one of them was ill this morning. How is she doing, do you know?"

"I never hear nothing, so she prolly all right. If they send an ambulance or something majors, I'd know about it."

"K.O., if you want to check on her before we go, we can do that," Melanie said.

K.O. smiled her thanks. Melanie guided her through the conference and meeting rooms, a small kitchen, and more lodgings. They exited a side door next to the recreation center.

"We even have a bowling alley here," Melanie said, as she opened a sound-dampening door. A rush of noise and activity greeted them. Several bowling lanes, a snack bar, a shoe rental area, and a separate arcade room were tucked in the back of the main building.

Teenagers—some K.O. recognized from the barracks, including Kimmy——laughed, bowled, chatted and ran around. As she watched individuals, she noticed a pattern to the chaos. The center of the whirlwind was a pale but upright Angela. Looking tired but pleased, she sat amid the noise and activity, like a queen whose subjects came to pay respects.

K.O. crossed to Jane. "Hi, there. Remember me? I'm K.O. from the barracks this morning?"

Jane smiled and nodded. "Of course."

"I see your patient has recovered."

"Yes. So it would seem." A raucous burst of laughter came from Angela's group. "She had me worried there for a while. I wanted her to stay and rest, but she said that was boring, so we made a deal. I let her come and hang here with her friends, as long as I was her chaperone, and she didn't bowl. As soon as 'Auntie Jane' says enough, she has to go back to bed. She's been good as gold.

"The other kiddos were really worried. Most of them have known each other for years, and someone—usually Angela—has a major medical episode each summer. Each year, Angela comes to us in worse shape than the year before. We get her stabilized and on a schedule, but as soon as she goes home to Molokai, it's off again. It's very remote where she lives, and she's a teenager. I don't think she tests her blood even once a day. I'm not sure how often she takes her insulin. She doesn't want scoldings, so she won't tell me the truth." Jane's short, red-blonde hair stuck up in tufts, and her pale skin and tightness around her eyes told K.O. how worried she really was.

"Let me know if there's anything I can do," K.O. said. "Melanie, the Supervisory ranger is taking me on a tour of Volcanoes, so I'll be gone most of today . . . Well, probably most of the time. I still may take you up on—" K.O. jumped back as a brief chase scene interrupted her speech. Kimmy pursued a young, handsome boy past them to the snack bar, and she called out "Hi!" to K.O..

K.O. laughed. "As I was saying. I'd like to come to the campfire one time if I can. Is it every evening?"

"Yes, at seven. We have stories, popcorn, juice. It's a nice, mellowing-out time. The younger ones go to bed right after that, and the teens stay up and talk until all hours. We have a curfew, but as long as they're in range, we don't get too *hu hu* unless somebody blows it. Anyway, the fire ring's out behind the building here. Follow the path out the barracks' door, and you'll run right into it."

"Thanks. I'll be seeing you." K.O. turned to find that Melanie had wandered off and was chatting with some teens by the snack bar. "Okay, I'm ready when you are."

"Okee doke. Let's go." Melanie showed K.O. yet another exit, and they passed a couple of old-fashioned gas pumps on their way back to the car.

They continued past the Jaggar Museum and an overlook.

"Some of this you can come back and do on your own. I want to finish the drive and have our picnic. By one, yeah?" Melanie asked, referring to the training session.

K.O. nodded.

They drove in silence for several minutes, K.O. taking in the hues of the landscape and the sounds carried on the clear air.

"Okay, this is the 1971 flow we're passing through. It converges with the 1921 flow. You might have noticed that when you entered the Ka'u desert on Highway 11, it had signs for other flows, too. Since the mountain is cone-shaped—Duh!"—Melanie laughed—"the same flow can take off in hugely different directions, and by the time it reaches the sea, its branches are miles apart."

She slowed. "Okay, this is the 1894 flow. See the different shades of gray, and the heavier undergrowth? *'Ohi'a* trees are always the first things to pop up after a fresh flow. The seeds need the heat to germinate. No wonder the darn things are so hard. You have to be tough to grow in a lava field. Look at the beautiful *lehua* blossoms!"

Bright red blooms, like Mainland bottlebrush, grew high in the trees.

"Now that"—Melanie waved her hand towards K.O.'s window, narrowly missing her nose—"is the turn off for Chain of Craters Road. We don't have time today, but you have to make time to get down there. It's totally awesome, and the scene of several of our incidents."

As she said this, Melanie lost her frivolous tour-guide persona. She took a deep breath and sighed noisily. To K.O., it seemed the weight of Melanie's job at the park had just resettled on her shoulders after a brief but welcome break.

They passed turn-offs and hiking trails to the smaller craters and the ash beds. The landscaping once again became lusher as they approached the tree fern jungle. Huge ferns, some towering many feet over the car, lined both sides of the road.

Melanie followed a turn-off for Thurston Lava Tube, and parked in the full lot behind a tour bus.

"Okay, here's our picnic spot. I'm starved, so let's eat and I'll show you the tube. It's really great." She retrieved the lunch and set off down a trail opposite the tube, overhung with greenery, keeping up a steady stream of chatter that K.O. let flow in one ear and out the other.

Now that K.O. was out of the car, she was able to see, hear and smell the uniqueness of the park. The trail was too short for K.O., and in only a few minutes they faced a vista of another, much smaller crater.

"This is Kilauea Iki," Melanie informed her. "Means Little Kilauea." A worn picnic table and a few benches, unoccupied, faced the crater overlook. "This flow is from 1959. It's kind of creepy, these recent flows so close to the park buildings. I mean, Hilo's right there, too. What if Madame Pele gets mad and shoots a river at the town?"

"It hasn't happened, yet, so don't worry." K.O., also hungry, began rooting in the backpack, pleased to note that Melanie had been kidding about egg salad for lunch.

"Oh, yes it has!" Melanie told K.O. about a lava flow that had threatened the town of Hilo, but had stopped just short when locals had made sacrifices to Pele and appeased her.

K.O. enjoyed their lunch and conversation.

"Time to see the tube, then get back to the office. And you have a session to give. I'm not going to be at all the sessions, but I'll attend what I can. I have a park to run, and I already have a reciprocal certificate."

Melanie returned the backpack to the car and led K.O. across the parking lot to the entrance of Thurston Lava Tube.

K.O. stepped inside the cool and dripping tube. Like a cave, but 400 feet long, it had formed when cooling outer lava formed a straw-shaped pipe. Molten lava had flowed through it until the source dried. The tube, now cold and lava-free, was artificially lit and hung with ferns and shadows. Although it was full of tourists, K.O. was able to separate herself from the side conversations, feel the chill air, and hear the sound of the tube itself.

A flash of white caught her eye. The butt of a handmade cigarette had been dropped in a niche in the tube. Even in the damp, she could smell the flakes of a high-grade *pakalolo*. An empty condom wrapper lay next to it. She pocketed both and continued down the tube and out the far end. Melanie, in her park uniform, held forth about the tube and the park for an ever-growing audience of tourists. K.O. smiled, listened a bit, and then stepped around to continue down the trail. A young man's question, however, stopped her.

"What about all that stuff we hear about Kona gold and Kona buds, Maui Wowie, like that?"

Melanie smiled. "For those of you uninitiated, this young man is referring to the special marijuana, for which our islands are notorious." Some chuckling came from the crowd. "I have to say, I don't know of any myself, although I'm sure it's everywhere, if you look."

"You mean, like growing wild?" He seemed excited at the prospect.

"No. We have a special task force for that. They do sweeps and wipe out any crops they find. What I meant was, although we don't openly advertise, it's in the islands, even this one, if you want it bad enough and know where to look." K.O. caught her eye. "I see my time is up, and it's been a pleasure to chat with you. Enjoy your time at Hawai'i Volcanoes National Park, and your visit to the islands. *Mahalo.*" She followed K.O. down the trail to the car.

"I think I might have a sample, if you care to add it to your next lecture," K.O. said, as she got in.

Melanie looked startled as K.O. pulled the butt out of her pocket.

"Where did you get that?"

"In the tube. And this," she said, as she pulled out the condom wrapper with a flourish.

"Oh, jeez." Melanie started the car and drove around the curves back to Volcano House.

"So, tell me about the crops here," K.O. said.

"We sure have them. We've cleared out a ton in the remote areas, but not recently. They doubled the force for that in recent years, and the park itself has remained clean. I'm sure someone just brought that into the tube for a quick jolly. You know, the risk of discovery, and all that."

"Maybe. Do you have information on recent harvests on park property? Maybe a map? What about any other labs on property? Weapons stashes?"

"Most people aren't that stupid. This is a National Park. To do something on the property makes it a Federal beef. Who wants that?"

"Yeah. But I'd like to check it out all the same. Cross check the statistics of violence and drugs or weapons, see if any light bulbs go off."

"I did that, oh . . . six months ago. I didn't find anything—but hey, a fresh pair of eyes is always welcome. I have all the arrest reports, etc. I don't have Federal reports. They do memos, because we don't 'need to know.' Sheesh." She pulled into the Military Rest Camp lot and stopped. "Here you go. Need anything?"

"Nope, I don't think so. I'll just grab my papers from my briefcase, and pray my supplies list was filled. If not, we wing it!" K.O. got out of the car and leaned in the window. "Thanks for the tour and lunch. Whenever you find the paperwork, I'd be happy to look it over."

She retrieved her materials and headed into the building, a little apprehensive about her first session. "Just first day nerves," she said to herself, as she opened the conference room door and found silent, unsmiling faces looking at her from twenty people seated in ranks of metal folding chairs.

Great. Just great.

CHAPTER TWELVE

Gerald and Jolene hunched over the plants in the lava tube. Many were growing well, but a few were still stunted, something that puzzled Gerald.

"Maybe the seedlings were inferior to start with," he mused.

"Shuddup already! Jeez, Gerald, you been goin' on like dis for one hour! Move on, brah. Help me."

"Okay, okay. I'm just trying to maximize the crop. After your screw up with Tommy, we can't afford any more mistakes. Where did you leave off?"

"I'm on dis bed, and I done dis section here." Jolene indicated the hydroponically equipped raised beds. "Just separate out da males from da females. We're behind 'cause of you. We shoulda been done by now."

"'Cause of *me*? How you figgah? I'm da one trying to make da bes' buds here. You doin' your hair or something half the time!"

"Gerald," she spoke softly, as if to an idiot, her pidgin completely evaporating. "There is a certain amount of loss in any crop. That is acceptable and expected. By wasting time on those plants that will never perform adequately, you waste my time, too, and Rudy's money. So, if you understand that fully, I suggest you move your ass, and see to the crop." She turned back to the plants and moved quickly, culling the males, so they wouldn't fertilize the females. Earlier in the growth, they had pinched off the top leaves to encourage branching, which increased the number of buds.

Jolene finished her task and moved to the inverted plants, hanging in the rear of the tube. "Ooh, these gonna be good ones, I can tell." She inhaled deeply. "Okay, you almost done, Einstein?"

"Yeah, yeah. What else we gotta do? Dis tube gives me da creeps out here."

"Rudy gave me money to buy da stuff for da catchment. So, we gotta dig where the pipes is gonna go. I got the system set up far from here, so we gotta hide da pipe between here and there."

Gerald stared at her, open mouthed. "You must be outta your mind! Dig through the lava? Lay pipe without anyone noticing? You using the product or what?" Gerald knew Jolene stole from Rudy periodically, but had never suggested he knew.

Jolene's eyes narrowed. "You don't know nothing, you Buddah-head, so keep your mout' shut, and maybe you see your cut at the end."

"My cut! That's a laugh. I can't wait for this cycle to be over, and then I'm outta here. You crazy, girl."

"You think you can just walk away? Wake up, little boy, you in dis 'til Rudy say you not. Den we see." Jolene exited the tube, and a halo of light framed her for a moment as she passed through the entrance.

Some angel, Gerald thought. He was beginning to think Jolene really was unstable, and not just putting on an act to keep her position in the "company." Glumly, he followed her back to the truck and followed her terse directions to the site of the catchment tank.

To her credit, Gerald was impressed with how invisibly the tank had been hidden, blending with the rock and vegetation. Even up close, the tank was undetectable, except for a small, well-camouflaged pipe that drained into it. Gerald followed the pipe, and one hundred yards away, found a cleverly concealed, roof-like, plastic corrugated platform that would catch and funnel water into the pipe. An overflow valve at the back of the tank allowed water to spill over, should heavy rains flood the system. Gerald turned to congratulate Jolene, and found her rooting through a pile of supplies partially covered by cammo netting and hidden by a deadfall.

"Good job. How did you manage by yourself?"

"Who said it was by myself? Help me pull this stuff out."

Gerald moved to assist. "But Rudy said we had to do it alone, since you, uh, disposed of Tommy, and he didn't want anyone else to know."

"Yeah, well. Nobody does know. Now. Take this." She handed him several sections of PVC pipe. Gerald didn't want to think of what might have happened to the help she had enlisted. Unbidden, his head replayed the small but solid "thump" of the machete embedding in Tommy's back, and Tommy falling at his feet.

Jolene was instructing him. ". . . and you take these sections and map a route to the tube. This is a gravity feed, so we don't need a pump, or more electricity. The geothermal set up for the Metal Halides is all we want, anyway. Just make sure you don't make any weird turns that stop the flow of water. You need to install a flow regulator at the tube, so the plants get water whether someone is there or not. Maybe some day we won't be here, but we have to protect the crop."

Gerald tightened his grip on the piping and swallowed. He was hired for a purpose, but this was all getting too nerve-wracking. It was starting to sound like the plot of a bad Godfather movie, and he seriously wondered about Jolene. Gerald was supposed to be the brains, and Tommy had been the muscle. Now it seemed like Jolene was both, and where did that leave him?

"How far are we in a direct line to the tube?" he asked.

"Somewhere between a quarter and half a mile."

"You're kidding! I'm supposed to dig a trench for this damn

pipe for half a mile through lava?"

"Do I look like I'm kidding? Get busy. I'm not doing everything myself. I'll tell you how to do it, and then you do it. Got it?"

Gerald nodded. For the next several hours, Gerald toiled in the lava, sometimes merely moving chunks, sometimes belly down, chipping with chisel and mini-sledge hammer to get the pipe buried deep enough. Jolene kept busy, too. Criticizing, nagging, complaining.

When she finally allowed him to stop, the sun was an orange ball, low in the sky. The pole-like trunks of the ʻōhiʻa trees stood straight and black—silent sentinels. The warm air smelled of dust and flowers.

Slowly, they disguised the evidence of their project, recovering the pipes and tools in the deadfall. To Gerald's grim satisfaction, the pile of supplies was noticeably smaller.

He was bloody where razor-sharp lava had sliced his skin and clothing as easily as a saw blade would. His body ached, and he stood hunched over, like an old man. Jolene was also filthy because she had fitted and glued the PVC together, made the connection to the catchment system, and pulled pipe for Gerald to lay.

Exhausted, they staggered to the truck and sat on the bench seat, doors open, and listened to the sounds of approaching night.

"I don't think I can do this again tomorrow, Jolene."

"Oh, yeah? So what you going to do instead? Watch the 'Bows on television?"

"You know I don't like local football. No, I don't think I'll even be able to push the button on the remote by tomorrow. I need to rest a day, and then I can work." He hated the pleading tone in his voice, but he couldn't help it. He hurt so much, he felt tears welling up as he fumbled for the ignition.

Jolene seemed to enjoy his tone and his discomfort. If she was in half the pain he was, she hid it well, he thought.

"Yeah, okay. Tomorrow, you stay home. You better not be off somewheres, 'cause I might stop by and check on you."

She would, too. But Gerald was sure that he wouldn't move the next day. "No problem. Use your key if you come by, 'cause I'm not answering the phone or the door."

He managed to start the engine and reverse out of the small clearing. No worries about tire tracks or footprints in the lava, he thought. Might need new tires after this, though. Business expense? He chuckled painfully at the thought.

"What's so funny?"

"Nothing. Just thinking about new tires for the truck after this."

"You're right. That's not funny."

Gerald drove slowly and carefully—the only way he could, without increasing the numbing heaviness in his body.

Jolene, far from pain-wracked, seemed to gain energy the farther they drove from the site. She fairly bounced in her seat, and bubbled with plans for the next day of work on the project. Gerald watched her manic movements, the gleam in her eye, and tightened his grip on the steering wheel. He felt the cuts on his damaged hands open again, warm blood trickling down the wheel and onto his wrists.

CHAPTER THIRTEEN

K.O. stepped up to the table at the head of the room and set her notes and displays down slowly and carefully, using the time to assess the mood of the room. No clue. She lifted her face to them with a bright, fake smile.

"Good afternoon. I trust you all had a good lunch and are ready for the introduction to the training?"

"We were ready twenty minutes ago," came a sour voice from the back.

K.O. glanced at her watch. It had stopped somewhere between Kilauea Iki and here. She had lost track of time, and one of her fears had come to pass: late to the first session. At least she wasn't naked—another of her fears, and the subject of many nightmares.

"I am so sorry." K.O. was genuinely chagrined. She hated to be late, hated to keep people waiting, or to be kept waiting, for that matter. "My watch seems to have stopped, and I know your time is valuable. I'm setting a terrible example, but I'll try to make it up to you. How's this? I'll talk fast, and you'll learn fast, and I won't have you stay twenty minutes later to make up for my mistake, okay?"

Her audience seemed to like that idea. They sat up more alertly, unfolded their arms, and relaxed their faces into more pleasant expressions.

"I see they've provided us with some water and juice, so please help yourselves any time. Unless we're working on defensive tactics." A few smiles appeared. *Okay, I'm not going to be flayed and tortured. Today.* "Has everyone signed in?" Mostly nods, with a few negative responses. She handed the clipboard to the nearest person, who passed it on.

"For the first session or two, until I get to know you better, I'd like everyone to wear a name tag. And to get things rolling, add your soap-opera name under it." She got some definitely puzzled looks. "I'm sure you were given that memo." She eyed them sternly, then heaved a mock heavy sigh. "Okay. Take your middle name as your first name, and your street name as your last name. If your street name is a number, then use the nearest cross street that isn't a number. If you don't have a middle name, use your first name backwards."

She watched people distribute name tags and pens, and then configure their "new names." Her ice-breaker activity was working. Now, genuine laughter filled the room, and people created soap-opera-like dialogues using their new identities. She circulated, addressing her charges by both their real names and their aliases. Her own, Anirtak Kahekili, was much admired. She asked them to come up with an occupation for their new character. K.O. said she was a spiritualist from Romania. She allowed the activity to build, and when it seemed to have peaked, she called the room to order, and focused on the first session.

The afternoon passed quickly, and the group bonded throughout. The only exception she could see was Clayton Hsu, who arrived even later than she had, and missed the soap-opera naming, and thus the camaraderie generated.

She finished her material early and released them a few minutes before the scheduled time. Several people approached her to say how much they had enjoyed the class and looked forward to future sessions.

K.O. packed up and left the room feeling successful. She had no dinner plans, and as she walked the short distance to her barracks, she thought about driving into the town of Volcano and having dinner there.

She opened the barracks door and again her ears were assaulted by noisy teenagers, only this time, it seemed familiar and friendly. Word had apparently spread, because she was greeted by name, and in between their finger sticks and blood testing, many kids came over to her.

Angela, who occupied the bunk above Kimmy's said, "Hi— K.O., right?"

"Yup, that's me."

"That's a cool name."

"Thanks. What are you guys going to do now?"

"Eat dinner, then have our campfire. Wanna come?"

"Jane invited me to the fire, and I might take you up on that." K.O. smiled at the girl, who seemed shy, but was making an effort.

"I heard you were there when I, um, was kinda comatose?"

"Yes. My first experience with that. And my first experience with thousands of teenagers." K.O. grinned, hoping to make the girl relax a little.

Angela smiled. "Don't worry, I'm fine. It happens all the time."

It does? But K.O. didn't say that aloud.

A young woman walked briskly down the center aisle, clapping her hands. "Okay, okay, you guys. Everybody tested?" A range of answers, all shouted at once. "If you're done, head over to the dining hall. Joe, stay with those who aren't, then walk them over."

K.O. saw the medical corner, as she mentally termed it, filled with equipment and several adults she presumed were nurses or doctors, because the group included Dr. Doug and Jane. The adults, except for the man called Joe, who sat with a small group, exited with the kids.

Angela slithered down onto Kimmy's bunk.

"What's up?" K.O. asked, noting the lack of testing equipment, or indication Angela would test.

"I got a bad feeling."

"You sick? I can get Joe. Or Jane."

"No. Not that. Sometimes I get feelings, you know? And they're almost never wrong. My Auntie, she stay one *kahuna*, and I get some *mana* from her."

"*Mana*, huh?"

"Yeah. Power, you know. Like one time, I knew my *halau* was goin' win at the hula festival, and we did."

"That's not really psychic."

"Yeah, but we only danced together two months, and had two beginners, *haoles!*" Angela's eyes widened as she described the unlikelihood of winning by a newly formed dance group, saddled with untrained Caucasians, no less.

"Okay, maybe kind of a miracle, but it's not a bad thing."

"They not always good things." Angela's voice was almost too low to hear.

"Okay, so what's the deal here? You think you might get sick again?" Angela shook her head. "I know. You didn't start off very well, and you're worried?"

A sob escaped Angela. "I don't even know you, and I'm talking to you."

"It's okay. Sometimes it's easier to talk to a stranger."

"Yeah. But that's not what I mean."

"Tell me, Angela. Maybe I can help."

"Something bad goin' to happen to you while you're here."

"What kind of something?"

"I not sure. Something with Madame Pele."

"What do you mean? Madame Pele?" Angela just shook her head. "Okay. Say she's real. She guards the volcano, right? What does she care about a *haole* visiting? I'm not going to take her lava—even I know that much. I'm not going to eat her *'ohelo* berries. Maybe I'll sacrifice the gin I got on the plane to her. She loves gin, yeah?"

Angela nodded. "It's going to be bad, but I can't tell what happens."

"Did you dream this?"

Angela's jaw hardened, and her lips puckered into a stubborn pout. "I *do* dream things. But this kind of dream is different. A vision."

K.O. sighed. How much of this was Hawaiian lore learned from an overzealous auntie, and how much was hormone-induced teenager-ness?

"Angela. What should I do to help you feel better? I won't do anything dangerous, okay? You may just be a very perceptive young lady. I have a confession to make. This job here at the park—I'm treating it like a vacation, but it's not." Angela's attention was focused on K.O., and the little-girl face was overlayed by a strange, older version.

"I had some bad things happen to me at work on Oʻahu before I came here. So, this job is kind of like a healing for me."

"I know. Your friend. She almost died."

K.O. gasped. "Who told you? I haven't told anyone here, not even the head ranger!"

"I told you. I know things." Angela's face resumed its thirteen-year-old roundness and innocence.

K.O.'s feet felt heavy—the familiar aftermath of an adrenalin dump that left exhilaration and exhaustion in its wake. "What was your vision, Angela?" K.O. asked dully.

"On the crater rim. The far side. An offering. Sacrifice, dancing, for you. All for you. To protect you."

Angela rose and left the silent barracks, the bang of the door the only sound.

K.O. sat unmoving on her bunk.

CHAPTER FOURTEEN

K.O. now felt no desire to leave the park for dinner. The rec room didn't offer much in the way of a real meal, so she decided to eat at Volcano House. She wasn't really in the mood to eat at all, after hearing Angela's vision—or whatever it was.

Who's to say what's real and what isn't? K.O. sighed.

She wearily headed back to the rental car, determined to eat a good meal and have an early night. She pushed all thoughts of Madame Pele, sacrifice, all that woo-woo stuff, to the back of her brain. Stay there, she told it.

Volcano House was bustling. A busload of tourists browsed in the gift shops and lined the waiting area. The sun was setting, and after K.O. put her name in for a table, she wandered out the back door to the same viewing area she'd used earlier. This time she sat on the wall, feet on the crater side, and although she tried to avoid it, her eyes were drawn to the site of her own vision—the Hawaiian procession on the far rim. Amid the noise and laughter, she felt unanchored, adrift. The breeze was brisk and cooling in the setting sun. She shivered and rose, deciding to wait inside, having neglected to bring a sweater.

She lifted her leg over the wall. Someone crashed into her and knocked her off-balance. She cried out, but before she could fall over the edge, a strong hand wrenched her back onto the patio, and she turned to face Clayton Hsu and Kamuela, the driver from the airport car rental.

"Oh, my God," she gasped. Sudden sweat beaded her forehead and quickly dried in the breeze. Feeling queasy, she sat on the wall again, both feet firmly planted on the cement.

"Sorry, sorry," said Kamuela. "Are you all right?" His face wrinkled with worry, and the familiar brown eyes met hers.

"Yes, I think so. What happened? Who pushed me?"

"Me. I did." Clayton nervously lit a cigarette and inhaled deeply. "I'm sorry." He didn't look overly sorry.

"What happened?" K.O. asked again.

"It was an accident. Someone pushed me, and I bumped into you." Clayton took another drag.

K.O. glanced to Kamuela for confirmation, but he was looking at Clayton.

K.O. stood. "So, Kamuela, you grabbed me?"

His eyes opened wide and his mouth dropped. "How do you know my name?"

Clayton froze, his cigarette mid-toke, eyes darting between them.

K.O. watched both men. Their reactions were interesting. "You drove me on the courtesy bus from Keahole airport to the car rental lot yesterday. What are you doing here?"

Her response seemed to put him a little more at ease. "Yeah, that's only part-time. I also drive a tour bus. I brought a busload up from Kona for dinner, then onto Hilo tomorrow." He grinned broadly. "What are you doing here?"

Now K.O. noticed his company aloha shirt, complete with name tag. Some detective. "You're also wearing your name tag."

Kamuela's dark skin went mahogany-red, as he glanced down, then laughed. "Sure, sure!"

"So, how do you know Clayton?" She kept her gaze on Kamuela.

"We don't really, that is, we—"

Clayton interrupted loudly, overriding anything Kamuela might have said. "We ran into each other here—you know, both being in the tour business."

K.O. folded her arms across her chest. "It's cold and I'm going back in. I'm waiting for a table." Tired of the game in which she wasn't included, she pushed past them and returned to the dining room.

"Is my table ready yet?" she asked the young woman at the podium.

"Just a few more minutes. We just got a large party and had to scoot over the last small table." At K.O.'s darkening scowl she added, "But I'm sure something will open up soon." She smiled and hurried away.

Sure, K.O. grumbled, they have the corner on the market. You gotta eat, there's no place else to go. She felt a gentle tug on her sore arm and whirled to find Kamuela behind her.

"I have a table you could share. I eat out the back door, but it's really pretty, and I'd like the company. Come on. Sorry about Clayton . . . Please?"

K.O.'s first instinct was to tell him where he could put his table, but then she thought better of it. She might get some information out of him. Clear up a few questions. He obviously knew Clayton Hsu better than he let on, and better than she did. Clayton seemed bound and determined to make her "easy" job as difficult as possible. And forewarned was forearmed, as they said.

She smiled engagingly. "Thank you for your kind offer. I accept both the apology and the table."

Kamuela looked startled at her rapid change of attitude, but rose to the moment, leading her out the side door and around to the employee dining patio off the kitchen—unoccupied at this time of the evening.

"Just let me tell them we're out here." Kamuela disappeared through the kitchen door and returned a moment later with menus and glasses of water. "I'll also be your server tonight, since everyone is busy with the rush, okay?"

K.O. nodded. "Clayton won't be joining us, I take it?"

"No." Kamuela glanced at his menu, then tossed it down and watched K.O. as she read hers.

"I'll have the large house salad with papaya dressing and the side of assorted rolls. Iced tea. Thanks."

Kamuela took the menus back to the kitchen. The door banged shut, muffling the noise. Full dark now, the huge, round moon lit her little alcove. The breeze was muted here by the building, and she wasn't chilled. She heard cars starting in the distant parking lot, and bits of conversation wafted to her. Her body relaxed. She hadn't realized how tense she had been. Her arm ached from the shoulder down, where Kamuela had pulled her back from the edge.

I probably wouldn't have fallen all the way to the bottom, she thought. *Just broken every bone in my body on the way through the bushes, trees, lava rocks and whatever else is down there. I wouldn't have to fall all the way to the bottom, just a few yards might have done the trick.* Fear trickled down her spine. The kitchen door banged open again, and Kamuela reappeared with her iced tea, a bottle of wine, two glasses, and a sheepish grin.

"Just in case you change your mind." He set the drinks on the table and sat down.

K.O. decided the wine looked pretty good and nodded when he offered her a glass. The day had caught up with her, and she rummaged in her bag for pain reliever.

"You look really wasted."

"Thanks."

"No, I mean . . . I'm sorry. Does your arm hurt?" He watched her down two pills with the wine. "Let me see." He came to her side of the table, and gently moved her arm into the angle of light coming from the partially open kitchen door.

He pushed back her sleeve and she gasped as he moved her arm again. He said nothing, but his touch was gentle, and after a moment, the pain subsided.

"I think it's just strained. Nothing broken or bruised on the outside. Should be fine tomorrow. Unless you're going to be doing gymnastics." He smiled. K.O. groaned. "What? Did I move it?"

"No. I teach Defensive Tactics tomorrow, so there's no way I can rest it. Maybe I can reschedule that for later in the week."

"What are you doing here? I'm guessing not a vacation?"

"No. I'm here to train the park rangers."

"Oh, you're a park ranger?"

"No. Just here for the training." She wasn't sure how much he knew, but didn't want to reveal her occupation if Clayton hadn't already told him. "So—how do you know Clayton?"

"Like he said, we're both in the tourist business." He didn't look at her, and she felt there was more to it.

"What happened with you two at the view point? Someone pushed me hard. It wasn't a bump from an off-balance tourist. What's going on?"

Kamuela sighed, then smiled. "I'll go check on dinner."

K.O. drank her wine, then poured more. Just as she was wondering about finding the bathroom, Kamuela reappeared with two laden plates and a basket of bread perched precariously between them.

K.O. had to smile. She relieved him of the bread and refilled his wine glass. They dug in. When K.O. was nearly finished, and had given up hope of learning more about her near-disaster, Kamuela did an odd thing. He reached across the table and took her injured arm in his two hands.

"I'm sorry about the push. I did it. Clayton admitted it, but I did it. I'm really sorry. He said it would be funny, a joke, and I went along with it. As soon as I did it, I realized how stupid it was. That's why I was close enough to grab you. You didn't even fall." K.O. remained silent, and he released his warm grip on her arm. He sat back and studied the moon. "Clay and I used to be buds, you know. He's gotten really stressed at this job, and he's trying to quit smoking." His voice drifted off. "When the NPS told everyone about this training thing, they were all excited. Clay too, for a while. He called his brother at Hilo PD and tried to get him this gig. Clay's always looked up to his big brother until he started screwing up. Clay wanted to follow him into police work, but couldn't for some health thing, so his big brother is like, living Clayton's dream. Come on." He pushed back from the table, led K.O. around the building to the wall on the crater, and sat.

"Anyway, things are going bad at Hilo PD. I think they're going to can Clay's brother. I don't know what Clay's going to do then."

K.O. looked at his profile. The silver moonlight spilled down his face, turning it into an ancient statue.

"I could really have gotten hurt. For what? A joke?" K.O. let the words float on the breeze over the crater. "Because you told me, I won't report you or Clayton to NPS. But I'm not going to put up with any more of his shit, either. You tell him to do his job, because I won't cover for him." And to change his clothes once a week would be nice too, but K.O. kept that remark to herself.

"Thank you." Kamuela leaned in and kissed her cheek. A gentle, feather-light, brotherly kiss. "I have much to atone for." He rose and stepped over the wall to the patio. "Dinner is on me. Get some rest. Keep this with you while you're here." He pushed a small, rough stone into K.O.'s hand, and curled her fingers around it. "Please." K.O. felt the sharpness of a piece of *aʻa* lava. She started to voice her thanks, but he had disappeared. She neither heard nor saw him go.

She heard a *mele*, an a capella Hawaiian chant, coming from the dining room, and remembered entertainment was provided on some evenings. A burst of applause broke the magic, and familiar strains of slack-key guitar picked up where the *mele* left off.

CHAPTER FIFTEEN

K.O. felt alone, encapsulated from the warm sounds of humanity drifting around her. The urge to fly over the crater surged through her and she shivered, turning away from the hypnotic view.

She retrieved her purse from the patio table and walked quickly to her car, deciding suddenly that she didn't want to be alone a moment longer. The obvious choice for company, wild and boisterous, was the dreaded fire ring. Teenagers, songs, popcorn—perfect antidote for her frayed nerves and tender arm. Come to think of it, it didn't really hurt any more since Kamuela had gently massaged it. No pain, but a sensitivity, an awareness of blood and bone.

At the barracks, she tossed her purse on her bunk and hurried down the trail to the fire ring. As she approached, she heard singing and smelled wood smoke. Rounding a bend, she came upon the group, seated on logs set in concentric semi-circles around a large stone-rimmed fire.

They had just finished "Swimming in the Toilet Bowl," when she arrived. Their burst of spontaneous applause startled K.O. She smiled and waved as Jane, Kimmy, and Angela scooted over to make room for her on a log. Jane stood and introduced her to more clapping and laughter. Someone handed her a cup of juice and a bowl of barbecued popcorn, unevenly popped, more like lumps of carbon than food. It had been years since she'd been to a campfire sing-along. Unexpectedly, she felt a lump in the back of her throat, and her eyes prickled with tears as she looked around at the smiling, happy faces—kids and adults alike. The feeling didn't last, however, because they began a leader-followers song, "Boota Hunt." The Hawaiian equivalent of going on a lion hunt—but for wild pig.

A large Japanese man K.O. heard called Dave, with the proportions of a sumo wrestler, stood backlit by the flames and proclaimed in a falsetto, "Two tissues! Pink kind! Sof' kind! Girl kind!" to the delight of the group, who repeated verbatim in word, tone and manner.

K.O. burst out laughing along with the others.

She felt a hand on hers and saw Angela had linked hands with Kimmy on her other side, too. K.O. felt Angela's trust and love, and squeezed gently. Angela smiled and squeezed back. Then they needed their hands for "swimming" during the Boota Hunt.

Half an hour flew by, and it was time to put the younger kids to bed. Younger being relative, as Jane explained. She herded the protesting kids back up the path to the barracks, calling to K.O., "If you want to sleep, don't come back for an hour!"

K.O. saw the older teens pair off or merge into smaller groups away from the fire. A few wandered off down the trail, and K.O. wondered if she should say something. She couldn't think of anything that wouldn't sound maternal or prissy, and then it was too late—she was alone on her log, staring into the lowering flames.

"Hi," said a breathless voice. K.O. nearly leaped off her log in alarm. How long had she sat unmoving? The fire was crumbled coals, and her body felt stiff and cold. She turned to see Melanie, still in uniform, seating herself on the log.

"Hi. You startled me."

"Sorry. Where is everybody?"

"The younger kids went to bed. The older ones all went off somewhere, and I didn't know if I was supposed to stop them, so, I just let them go."

"That was probably best." Melanie smiled. "Now you'll be their friend for life because you didn't try to *tell* them what to do! Not that they'd listen, anyway."

"They seem like a good group of kids."

"They are. So. How was your first session?"

"I was late. Not a good start."

"Oh, no! I thought we watched the time pretty closely."

"We did, but my watch stopped." K.O. glanced at her watch. "It's working now, though."

"I've broken three watches in the last two months, so I stopped wearing one. I decided somebody doesn't want me to tell time." Melanie's tone was bantering, but K.O. saw something else in her face.

"Anyway, the session was a good one, and I made up for being late by letting them out early."

"I wish I'd had teachers like you in high school!"

"Me, too."

"How'd you manage that? Will you have to make something up?"

"No. They opted to skip the afternoon break and just run to the bathroom when they needed to, so we covered all the material. I'm glad. It's been kind of a hectic first day."

Melanie studied her, and K.O. met her gaze. "Anything I can do to help?"

"I'm wondering what the story is with Clayton Hsu. He seems so . . . difficult. Why is he kept on? He was late today, by the way. I didn't dock him because he only missed the ice-breaker activity, not the actual session."

"And besides, you were late too, and how would that look?" Melanie laughed.

K.O. blushed. "Yeah, that, too."

"Clayton Hsu," Melanie whispered and sat silent. She tossed a stick onto the coals, sending up a shower of sparks. K.O. shifted uncomfortably on the log. Her butt hurt.

Melanie cleared her throat. "Clayton Hsu is technically my boss. He's the Operations Manager, and oversees the day to day running of the business end of the park, while I oversee the rangers." She sighed. "He's been here ten years. I've watched him go from an enthusiastic young executive-type, to this sort of, run over, beaten down, angry man you see. It's so sad."

"What happened? Do you know?"

"He's very private, but from what I gather, it's been a series of downturns. I guess first, he didn't really want the job. He wanted to be a police officer. Didn't make the cut. Took this job to be near his family in Hilo. Older brother's in Hilo PD, but I understand he is having some problems. Clay worships his brother. Then when Clay's son was two, he was diagnosed with autism. Strike three, his wife left him, went to the Mainland, saying she couldn't handle having a 'retard' for a son. Good riddance is my opinion."

K.O. nodded in agreement.

"Clay's been raising his son, with his family's help. Darien goes to a special day school, does real well from what I understand. He's high-functioning, but still, it must be a strain. I think Clay feels trapped here. He does his job well, but it's not his dream work. I feel sad for him, because my job *is* my dream work."

Again, K.O. nodded in agreement. She loved her job, especially since she had made arrangements to move laterally to Evidence. At times, she felt positively giddy with the possibilities of that new post.

"And as for why he is kept on, I don't know. You wouldn't think we'd have anything in common, but I feel as though we do. That's why I haven't reported his attitude to our superiors. He doesn't deal with the public, and for the most part, he does his job and really does take care of the people here. Something about

Volcanoes National Park works for him. Not his position here, I mean, but the park itself. It does for me, too. And for most of the people who stay on working here, year after year. Madam Pele takes care of us." Melanie laughed weakly, then stopped when K.O. didn't join in.

"Something is here," K.O. said softly. "I don't know what, but you can't stand on this ground, feel the pulse of lava running under your feet, see new land created in front of you, and not feel power. Not feel insignificant in the face of that power. And yet . . ."

"What?" Melanie barely whispered.

K.O. turned to face her. "And yet, know that if you needed that power, it would run right through you, feed you, push you, give you life." K.O. turned bright red at this sudden baring of her soul. Why had she said that?

Just as she was readying to discount her words, Melanie said, "Yes."

And that was all, but it held all the support K.O. could have wanted.

Both women seemed suddenly embarrassed at their exchange.

K.O. rose. "Well, time I got myself to bed. I hope the tiny teens are asleep by now." She checked her watch. "Damn. It's stopped again. Does the office or the gift shop have watch batteries?"

"I think so. If not, someone's always running into town for something. I'll leave a note on the message board."

Melanie walked into the shadows, and K.O. heard water running. Melanie returned with a bucket of water and poured it over the remains of the fire. She spread the coals out and repeated watering them. When she was satisfied the fire was out, she turned to K.O. once more. "Good night. Maybe you're not so *haole* after all." Melanie disappeared into the darkness.

K.O. stared for a moment, straining to hear Melanie's footsteps, but hearing only the night. She headed up her own trail to the barracks and to bed.

CHAPTER SIXTEEN

First light found Gerald hobbling from his bed in his tiny garage apartment to the bathroom-a distance of only a dozen feet, but it brought tears to his eyes and gasps of pain. His arms, hands and knees were black and blue, scabs like map-lines running across his skin. Back at his bed, he fumbled for the pain reliever in his nightstand. Normally using it only to stave off or reduce a hangover, he gratefully gulped several pills and flopped, groaning, back onto the rumpled sheets. He knew he couldn't sleep again until the pain was deadened, at least a little. He stared at the spider-shaped watermark on the ceiling and tried to breathe evenly. He drifted off.

A rustling among his papers, and the familiar sound of the truck keys ticking together woke him. Groggily, he focused on Jolene, as she opened his wallet and poked through it. He didn't react as she sat on his bed, but her weight on the mattress pulled uncomfortably at his aching muscles. He was marginally pleased that he didn't shriek in agony in her presence. Maybe the pills had kicked in. Jolene still said nothing, just stared at him. He checked the time: 10:17. He felt he could sleep for hours, but not with her sitting there.

"What?" he finally asked. She was wearing jeans and a long-sleeved Local Motion T-shirt. Maybe she was as scraped up as he was. Didn't seem to be in any pain, though.

"Just waiting for you to get up so we can get to work."

"What?" He could not have heard right.

"Move your ass. We've got pipe to lay."

"But." He swallowed the sudden huge lump in his throat and tried again. "But, remember? We were going to rest today. You *said.*" He sounded like a petulant first grader.

"Yeah, well, the plan's been changed. Get dressed." When he lay there unmoving, she flipped the covers off and slapped his legs off the bed. Unresisting, his legs hit the floor, and pain resonated up his spine. He moaned.

"Get up. You need help? Cheez." Jolene grabbed jeans and a T-shirt and thrust them at him. "I'm not dressing you. I'll be in the truck. You got five minutes."

She slammed the front door, her dark braid swinging, putting Gerald in mind of a gallows rope. Slowly he slipped one leg into the pants and bit back a gasp.

Four minutes later, dressed, out the door and panting, he struggled to raise his leg to the running board of the truck, pulling on the steering wheel to get in.

Jolene had taken the keys with her, which was why he'd not been able to find them. She had turned the ignition and cranked up the radio, Cecilio & Kapono wailing in the clear air. "Let's go. Move it. Rudy guys got a new project for us, and we gotta finish the catchment today and get the first crop ready to go." She drummed her palms against her thighs and jiggled impatiently.

Gerald started the truck and drove slowly, moving as little as possible, despite Jolene's increasingly bitter harangues about his incompetence. He pulled into the site as the sun reached its zenith. Sweat poured from him as he exited the truck. Before he started to work, he popped several of the pain pills he'd had the foresight to stash in his pocket.

* * *

The day dawned bright and clear for K.O. in the barracks. No dreams, no interruptions. Even the teenagers had had a good night from what she could tell. No medical emergencies. She was surprised to find the kids' exuberant presence a comfort and somehow already familiar. She accepted their invitation to join them for breakfast before her all-day training session.

She had managed to inform everyone of the schedule change from Defensive Tactics to Drugs & Weapons, and Field Intervention and Defusing. She thought she might test them on rescues, and throw in a little first aid. She wasn't too thrilled with another all-day, outdoor session as her only substitute for Defensive Tactics, but it seemed that busloads of students and artists were arriving today, and all the conference rooms were booked. Since she'd been scheduled for an outdoor session, she would have to stick to it.

I doubt if I'll be able to take it easy, but at least I can talk more and use my shoulder less, she decided. Her shoulder wasn't too bad, today. A little stiff, but that should go away with movement. She tested the arm and found it sore, but entirely useable.

The dining area of the barracks complex was as serviceable and unadorned as the sleeping quarters, except for a large fireplace at one end, with a cranky-looking stuffed moose head mounted over it. Go figure, she thought as she eyed it eyeing her. No moose in Hawai'i. It's probably mad that it's not in a bar in Alaska.

She moved down the food line, waving and calling to kids she recognized. Jane sat with the other adults this time, and waved her over. K.O. shook her head and pointed to Kimmy and Angela.

"Hi," K.O. greeted the girls as she set her tray down. "May I join you?" Nods and giggles. "So, how are you this morning?"

"Good," said Kimmy.

"Pretty good," said Angela.

"Everybody sleep okay? I did. Like a log."

"What are you going to do today?" Kimmy asked.

"Oh, some work stuff." K.O. dodged the question and sipped her coffee. "Bleah! They sure could use me to make their coffee."

"Put more sugar in it," advised Kimmy.

"I use the pink stuff. Don't like to add sugar."

"We *have* to use the pink stuff." Kimmy's lips poked out in a pout.

Angela reached over and tweaked her lip. Both girls laughed.

"My dad used to say, 'Stick that lip out any farther and you'll trip on it,'" said K.O.

"Mine, too!" said Kimmy. Then she sobered. "I hate not being able to eat what I want. It's just so hard, sometimes."

Angela nodded.

"I mean, it's embarrassing at school to test my blood. Or if I get low sugars, I sweat and shake, and everyone looks at me. If they don't know me, I hear them say I must be on drugs." Her eyes filled with tears, and she sniffed.

Angela handed her a paper napkin and she blew her nose.

K.O. said, "I don't have any medical thing like that to worry about myself, but I know a little about the strain of taking care of someone else. My dad had cancer, and I took care of him after his operation, until he was well enough to go home. Everything had to be done just right, or you could make things worse." Both girls nodded, breakfast forgotten. "And you know, it's my dad. I worried. Lost a lot of sleep, too."

Why am I telling them this? Two little girls? She looked at them. Kimmy's hair hung in a dark curtain hiding her face as she toyed with a piece of toast. Angela had her wiser-than-her-years face on. "Anyway, we're bringing this party down, girls. I gotta go soon, so let's talk about something else, okay?"

"I'm going to get some more coffee." Kimmy took her cup and left the table.

"So, Angela, what are you guys up to today?"

"We're supposed to see the baby nene geese. I can't wait. They're so cute."

"Where's that?"

"The park has a protected area where the nene can get away from mongooses and stuff. Not for tourists." She lowered her voice. "Jane's cousin works here and got us permission to visit!" Her eyes lit up and she was a child again. "Then we're having a workshop on '*Diabetes and Teenagers.*' Yuck. I bet they make us hike after lunch," Angela added morosely.

K.O. laughed. "You make it sound so exciting."

"Yeah, well, I'm not much of a hiker."

"Hey!" someone standing in the doorway called out. "Someone named K.O. in here?" He sounded puzzled, as if the name could not possibly be right.

K.O. stood. "Here."

"Phone call. Take it at the desk. This way."

K.O. hurried to catch him as he waved vaguely towards an open door. She entered a small office with an old black phone amid the papers on the desk. She picked up.

"Ogden, here."

"K.O.? You sound so . . . official."

"Alani!"

"Aaaagh! Calm down; my ear!"

"Sorry. I just wasn't expecting you to call. You're not here already are you?"

"That's a nice welcome. What if I am?"

"I'm sorry. I didn't mean it that way. I mean, I want to see you, but I just got started, and . . . well, the job is a little more complicated than I expected." Silence. *Great. My first date-like experience in *way* too long and I'm offending him. Way to go, Ogden.* "Alani?"

"Why does that not surprise me?"

He was laughing, damn it! "Stop laughing. I just got here. I haven't had time to create the problem, I'm just here to help with it."

He was definitely laughing, and so hard that he couldn't speak for a moment. "Okay. I'm sure there's time for you to get to that."

"That's not very nice."

He turned contrite. "I'm sorry, K.O.."

She loved how he said her name. Soft and warm and sexy like that. It made her think of . . .

"K.O.?"

"What?"

"What do you think?" *Rats. Must have missed something when I was picturing him paddling. Strong back muscles pulling at the paddle as he reached forward, the koa biting into the waves, the canoe surging ahead, pulling back, surging again . . . I've got to stop this.* She blushed and turned her back to the door.

"I, uh," Caught. "Say it again? I was distracted." *That's for sure.*

"I was saying, I missed you and wondered if the weekend might be a good time for me to come out? I have folks in Hilo to see, and I could stay at Volcano House, too. Do you think you'll be done by then? We can drive back to Kona together and see some of my friends before we come back to Honolulu. What do you think?"

K.O. calculated quickly. Today was Tuesday. Three more days of training, then maybe an extra session or two, but really, she should be done by Saturday noon at the very latest. "Sounds great. Saturday? Meet me in the dining room of Volcano House. We'll have lunch."

"Yes. Lunch sounds perfect." His voice, so warm, wrapped her, cradled her.

She sat on the desk with a thump, her knees suddenly weak. Maybe I won't show him the park after all, she thought. Maybe we should go straight to his room. I'd like to show him that. *Stop that!*

"Okay, then," she said softly. She heard the teens clanking and banging around the dining room, voices receding and doors slamming as they started their day. "I better get to work. I'm so glad you called."

"Me, too. I just needed—wanted to hear your voice. I know it's only been a few days, but . . ." he trailed off. "I'm getting ahead of myself." He became brisk, business-like. "I'll let you get back to work."

"Okay. Thanks."

"K.O.?" Soft again.

"Yes?" she squeaked.

"See you soon. Bye."

Good thing he hung up, because I haven't the breath to speak, she thought. Still hearing Alani's voice, she turned to go and was startled to see Angela in the doorway. How long had she been standing there? What did she hear? K.O. blushed furiously.

"K.O.?"

"Hey, Angela, what's up?"

"He might be the one."

"Who might be what one?"

"The Hawaiian guy on the phone. He might be the one."

Okay, Angela might have overheard enough to deduce a man on the other end of the call, but no way could she have known he was Hawaiian. A chill traced her spine as K.O. faced her. "Did you come here to tell me that?"

"No. That was just a little extra vibe. Threw it in for free." Angela's eyes twinkled.

"You're yanking my chain, girl!" She looped an arm over Angela's shoulder. "Shouldn't you be viewing ducks or having a workshop or something?"

"In a few minutes. I just came to tell you something."

"Yeah, well you already blew me away. Go for it. Walk me to the barracks. I gotta get my stuff." K.O. steered Angela, arm still over her shoulders, to the quonset hut.

"Something's going to happen out there. Today."

"What kind of something?"

"You'll be on the lava. Be careful."

"Not the fresh lava. We're not going there. Don't worry."

"I don't know exactly. But something."

"Okay, I'll be careful." K.O. stopped and faced the girl, both hands on her shoulders now. "I know you're worrying about me, but I'm not sure you should. I've been doing this a long time. *And I know how to take care of myself in dangerous situations.* Really, nothing is going to happen. It's just training. And in an emergency, if someone gets hurt or sick, I'm trained for that, too."

"Okay." Angela hugged her tightly. K.O. felt a jolt run the length of her body. Angela released her and ran back towards the main building. K.O. was left standing with the image of a curtain of fire running towards a pool of flame, and the coppery taste of fear in her throat.

CHAPTER SEVENTEEN

K.O. forced herself into the barracks to collect her daypack for the training hike. She included a first aid kit, water, sunscreen, and hat. She debated taking a weapon. She'd brought her off-duty .38 out of habit, but really hadn't thought she'd need it. She strapped on the ankle holster under her jeans pant leg, grabbed up the pack and a sheaf of training documents, and hurried back to the lodge.

In the conference room, the waiting staff had the air of an impending campout, rather than a training.

Good news, I guess, she thought. At least they think this is fun.

"Good morning, everyone." She called them to attention and took roll. "Thank you for being so flexible. We have a lovely day for our outing. The morning session will be outdoors, but we'll focus on your problems here at the park and some techniques to handle them. Questions? No? Okay, quickly, make sure you all have a first-aid kit, water, sunscreen, and a hat." Grumbling. "Yeah, I know, but do it anyway." Laughter and shoving as extra supplies were loaded and inventoried.

"I have presents for you all," K.O. called over the noise. "Here, take one, and pass the rest." She handed out packages of king-sized candy bars, to the delight of her charges.

"You're gonna look real good on the evaluation!" someone yelled out.

"That's my goal! Okay. We ready to roll?" Nods of assent. "Take a packet of training papers, 'cause I'm not carrying them all." She passed those out as well. "Drivers, raise your hands, please. Okay, everyone, saddle up. We'll meet on Chain of Craters Road, near the top, just before the cliff descent, for the first session. Hit the cans, whatever, and plan to start in thirty minutes. I'm driving too. Anyone need a lift?" No one did.

As people shuffled towards the doors and the parking lot, K.O. threw the extra water bottles and snacks into a box and carried it to her car. As she started the car and pulled out of the space, Melanie jogged up.

"Hey, can I catch a ride?"

"Sure, where to?"

"Observatory."

"Hop in."

Melanie got in and K.O. pulled onto Crater Rim Drive along with her trainees and a number of tourist vehicles.

"How will you get back?" K.O. asked.

"Someone will give me a lift."

"What's your hurry?" K.O. noted her fidgeting and restless energy. "Tourist uprising at the observatory?"

"No. That's not open to the public. I'll tell, but keep it under your hat, okay?" K.O. nodded. "We're getting an increase in activity."

"By 'activity,' do you mean the volcano? Like, eruption?" K.O. felt her palms slicken with sweat on the steering wheel. She thought she felt the road shift under the car, but that was probably her imagination.

"Yes. Our team is out on the flow now taking samples, but it doesn't look good. Activity has been increasing steadily for some time now. The seismographs have recorded an increase in the swarms of minor earthquakes, and the volcano's swelling. Pele's up to something. We may have to close public access to the flow. Bad for business. We're going out tonight to check. You should come. It's beautiful out there."

Yeah, and die in the dark. Swarms of earthquakes? Volcano *swelling*? "Uh, thanks. I might be busy with the training gig. Some other time." Over my dead body.

"We're gonna be out there every night, and every day for that matter, so join us if you can. You don't want to miss a chance like this."

Yeah. Right. "Here we are." K.O. slipped into a parking space fronting the observatory.

"Thanks, K.O. Have a good day. I'll catch up with you later if I can. Give you the scoops. Oh, your group's not going down to the flow today, are you? We're setting up barriers until we know for sure."

"No, we're at the top of Chain of Craters 'til noon, and then we go to the upper park, out in the sticks for some rescue stuff." Melanie nodded and waved, then disappeared into the building.

K.O. reversed and sped on to the meeting place. When she arrived, she saw her charges milling about, laughing and talking, flipping through the stapled handouts.

"No studying up ahead of time," she called to them. They gathered around her as she led them to some picnic tables. For the next hour, they discussed the current problems at the park, and how to improve the way they were handled.

After that, she instructed them in weaponless defense, take downs, and searches, amending her original plan. Her students were eager, and she felt an urge to condense her program, to speed their learning. Most of them had not had police training, and this was all very new to them. At one point she let them frisk her, and after everyone had had a go, she still had three potential weapons. She scolded the men for being too shy.

"It's not a date," she said, to their discomfort and the women's amusement. "We're talking about your life, here." She saved one goody for next to last. She opened her purse, packed especially for this training, and showed them a lipstick case. "You left me with this." The group knew something was up, and looked at each other questioningly. She removed the cap and swiveled up not a lipstick, but a small knife. "I could do some damage with this."

Last, she took them to her car to practice vehicle approaches. She set the scenario.

"Okay, I'm driving, either doing something you want me to stop, like speeding, or maybe my car matches a description of someone you're looking for. You've pulled me over, and one at a time, you're going to approach the vehicle to talk to me. After I speak to you, you're to continue walking to the picnic tables, and say nothing until I get out and join you. Understood?" Nods. "Make a line here. Wait until I'm seated, then approach the car, like you would to ask for I.D."

K.O. readied herself in the driver's seat, left elbow casually resting on the open window frame. She had brought a dud-weapon for this, an impressive-looking .357, incapable of firing. She rested the tip of the barrel in the crook of her left elbow, completely invisible to an approaching officer until too late.

The first person approached. She saw it was T.J., a more field-experienced ranger.

"Excuse me, ma'am," he began, then saw the weapon.

"Bang, you're dead," K.O. said softly.

T.J.'s face went sheet-white. He involuntarily clutched his stomach, but his back was to the waiting group, and K.O. was glad they saw nothing. He stumbled off to the picnic table. K.O. knew well the feeling he was experiencing, because it had happened to her the first time she had done this drill at the police academy.

She did the same to each member of the group, until they all sat, sober and silent at the picnic tables.

K.O. put her prop away and joined them.

"What do you think?" she asked them. No response for nearly

a minute. She knew what they thought. Mortality had popped up in their backyard. She felt for them, especially for T.J. and Jody, whose own mortality had come into play too recently.

To her surprise it was Clayton Hsu, who had been remarkably well-behaved throughout, who spoke first. "I am thinking, I would be dead."

"Yeah."

"Me, too."

"Shit."

"I read something like this happened to a police officer in California somewhere. Until now, I thought this training was a game. I see we have a lot to learn." Miranda someone from sales? Marketing? K.O. couldn't remember.

"I'm glad you're taking this seriously," K.O. said. "I'm sorry to put it out there like this, but violence is a reality. Anybody else want to say anything?"

Jody raised a pale hand.

"Yes, Jody?"

"Teacher, can we have lunch and recess now?"

The group burst out laughing and K.O. shouted, "Chocolate for all!"

Instead of going to the upper park, the site of their afternoon session, the group opted to eat where they were. K.O. thought it was because they didn't want to break up into the cars again after their experience. They needed a little time to get their equilibrium back. In an hour, she'd have them back off-balance, worrying, working, learning. She felt strongly about her responsibility to prepare them as thoroughly as possible for the absolute unknown. She joined them at the table, discussing vehicle approach, interview techniques, and answering questions, but noticed they kept one wary eye on her. Just as well. Learn it now, she thought, before you need it.

CHAPTER EIGHTEEN

Vastly cheered by lunch and chocolate, K.O.'s group got back into their carpools and drove to the next spot. She had told them where it was, as described by Melanie, and only a few old hands knew the location. Even she didn't really know, despite the map. She'd first heard about the land north of the park from Alani, who mentioned he had family who hunted there.

Alani. Her heart pitter-patted at the thought of him. *Focus. He'll be here this weekend, and I just won't think about it until then. Much. Got my hands full, anyway. Training, the problems at the park, and now, a possible eruption. It just gets better and better.*

She followed the caravan many miles to a remote pull off. She stretched as she got out of her tiny car.

"Is this even in the park, still?"

"Barely," answered Jody. "This is the boundary, but we never come here. We're usually too worried about the tourists and the flow and stuff."

K.O. saw that Jody's pale complexion was pink, despite the sunscreen he slathered on every hour. *I'm Irish,* she thought, *but this is ridiculous.*

She clapped her hands. "Okay, folks. Last session for today. Do good, and there's more chocolate for you!" The group gathered good-naturedly, but she saw they were weary.

She had set her scenario with Melanie's help, but no one else knew. "We're here all alone," she lowered her voice to an ominous whisper, "and a drug deal has gone down. I have roles for each of you." She passed out slips of paper on which she had written, "drug dealer" or "injured person" and her personal favorite, "hero."

"Don't tell who you are, specifically, we'll find out. In real life, the bad guys don't wear name tags." People chuckled as they read their assigned parts. "Here are some props." She passed out a few paper bags with various items in them, unknown to the group at large. "Don't tell what's in your bag, either; it'll give you away." Now people laughed as they pawed through the contents of their bags and got into the spirit of their secret roles.

K.O. had spent many hours in preparation, trying to make another dull service training a little different, and maybe fun. She had points to make, as in the vehicle approach workshop, but she also wanted them to come together as a staff, not just clerical vs. admin vs. rangers, as she'd seen in so many other trainings. Even in her own department, clerical, staff, and administration didn't always bond in a way that would make things move as smoothly as possible.

"Here is the current scenario. We're in the middle of nowhere. A drug deal has gone bad, intercepted by park staff. You each have a role, and you have to stick to that, no matter how much you might want to do something else!" She eyed Jody sternly. She had intentionally cast him as the drug lord, the head honcho, and she relished his discomfort as he grappled with this contrast to his ranger/helper image. Jody gave her a small smile and a nod

Hmmmm. Very interesting, K.O. thought. *Doesn't seem that out of sorts. Can't wait to see what happens next.*

"We have a framework, but no script. So, if something unexpected happens, go with it!" She glanced at her watch. "We have an hour for this, and then a debriefing. This is a traveling deal, so head south until we hit the cabin. Ready? Go!"

Her group immediately rummaged in bags, segregated themselves into good-guys and bad-guys, put on costume pieces and "injuries." She reveled to see how thoroughly they threw themselves into the activity.

Shouting from the trees gave way to a fist fight; the "drug-dealers" disagreeing on payment and quality. K.O. hopped on a fallen log to watch. Jody mock-slapped the woman from accounting for sassing him about his operation, and she immediately smeared some fake blood on her face. A group of men ran out of the trees, wielding sticks for knives and guns. They argued about their stash, then took off running down a lava-tumbled wash, as a group of men and women shouted, "Stop, you're under arrest!" and tried to cut them off.

"That always works," mumbled K.O., following the noise and crowd down the wash. When she caught up, out of breath, a melee had ensued, half real frustration, half laughter. Arrestees were on the ground, in hand-cuff position, and others—K.O. could not tell which "side" they were on—ran around the group, taunting and shoving.

Miranda enthusiastically searched Jody, who turned deeper and deeper shades of red. A scream echoed during the activity.

"I twisted my ankle!" "I've been shot!" "I've got a knife wound!" were the calls from the "injured" players.

"Okay, hustle, hustle," K.O. called. "Get the portable stretcher, wrap this ankle." She continued to encourage and monitor, and the group moved as a cohesive unit, tending to the wounded players. "Stabilized?" she called. "Arrestees under control?"

The entire group continued down the wash towards their destination. As K.O. shouted encouragement to the sweating, swearing staff, she jogged as best she could on the rough lava. Passing a wide spot in the wash, she caught a glimpse of something white, long and straight—and—*was that movement?*

Unsure, K.O. kept her focus on the team, and was soon far

away.

* * *

With the engine off, Jolene fell silent, too. She strode to the pile of supplies and gestured for Gerald to get busy. She immediately began to haul PVC and tools down the line of completed irrigation pipe. Gerald followed more cautiously,

The first hours passed agonizingly slowly as he and Jolene transferred the supplies to the area where they would work. By mid-afternoon, Gerald's body had either loosened up or given up, and he moved with much less pain. He knelt, mini-sledge and chisel ready, dreading another minute, much less another day of arm-wrenching, back-breaking labor.

An object smacked him in the head. Not hard, but startling. He looked up in time to see another Jolene threw at him. Kneepads. He smiled his thanks, but Jolene had already turned away and was eyeing the line. He bent to put them on.

He raised his chisel to make the first cut of the day, when from behind him in the brush, he heard voices raised in panic, and running footsteps. Then a large group of people ran right by him.

His mouth agape, he glanced at Jolene, farther along in the bushes. Also caught unaware, her mouth mirrored his own, but she recovered first.

"Get up! Get up! Take your tools!" she hissed.

He snatched up his supplies and dived for cover. Jolene rammed the glued pipe she held into the bushes and grabbed the loose sections, tossing them over a large lava mound, out of sight. "Shit! Shit! What the hell was that?" She scooted around behind the pile and joined him.

Gerald shook his head. "You see one guy on a stretcher? Wonder what happened?"

"Idiot! It doesn't matter what happened. We almost got caught! And why were there twenty of them? You see that lady? Like she was in charge, kept saying, 'Hurry up, he's been shot,' and something about disarming or something."

Her lips trembled, and Gerald smelled her sweat. They crouched together, cramped and frozen for many minutes.

"You think they're coming back?" Gerald finally asked.

"I don't know. Do I look like I know? We're miles from anybody. Where the hell did they come from?" She poked her head out from behind the lava, then stood. "Come on. We might not finish today like we should, but we gotta work a couple more hours."

Gerald slowly rose, feeling weak from the rush of near-discovery combined with his already sore body. He watched Jolene retrieve her pipe and continue as before, ignoring him.

"Bitch," he mumbled as he carefully lay flat, face down on the lava, and began to pound the chisel. The a'a slowly cut into his jeans, tearing fabric, then skin. He didn't notice.

CHAPTER NINETEEN

K.O. praised her exhausted group of "rescuers" and dismissed them immediately.

"We still have to debrief, but we can either do that in the Volcano House bar, or tomorrow in the regular workshop," she told them.

"Fo' reals?" T.J. asked.

"Yeah, I'm serious." K.O. laughed at his expression.

"Kay den! You're on. Right, guys?" Nods and chuckles as they staggered to their cars.

"You guys clean up and meet back at Volcano House . . . like an hour? How's that?" K.O. told them.

Some called, "See you." A few just waved, weakly.

K.O. policed the area, picking up rubbish and collecting the leftover supplies: a bottle of sunscreen here, a fanny pack there.

The sky was heavy and orange in the west, gray and thick to the south of her where toxic gases, released from the many vents in the mountain, spiraled upward in beautiful silver dances lit by the setting sun.

She drove slowly on the unfamiliar road. The afternoon workshop had run north of Highway 11, and the track she was on would eventually intersect Mauna Loa Road. Camping, hiking, and views were offered in this remote and pristine wilderness.

"I just wish I could see where I was going," she muttered, as yet another sidetrack looked promising. "I should have followed somebody. I don't know what the hell I'm doing." She talked to keep herself company, the radio useless in the rock-strewn area.

She came to a dead end, but recognized it as a section of the wash her crew had bolted down today during the "rescue."

She laughed as she remembered how everyone had gotten so into character. The four-person stretcher-bearers nearly dumping their patient, who ironically, really had turned her ankle, but no one had paid attention because they were so keyed up. The ankle had been taped "fo' real" as Jody would say, and the patient was fine—would even join them for de-briefing in the bar.

"I better get going." K.O. reversed in tiny increments until she was nearly turned around. Her eye caught a flash of white, and she was reminded of her earlier sighting in the dry lava-wash. She pulled the car as close to the edge as possible, nearly against a pile of rock and fallen 'ohi'a, and got out to take a look.

She walked into the headlights' glow and found an aluminum Hawaiian Sun juice can. "That's all. But I thought. . ." She shook her head. "Now I'm seeing things." She blew out a breath and returned to the driver's seat, carefully reversing again, and immediately finding the correct track to the main road. "I'm more tired than I thought." She peered out at the pitch black, unlighted, but paved road and tightened her grip on the wheel.

When she reached Highway 11, she breathed a sigh of relief and realized she'd been holding her breath. A few minutes later, she parked at the barracks and headed for the showers. Fortunately, the teenagers were already at dinner, and she had the place to herself.

A short, hot shower and a quick assessment of her scrapes and bruises. "Man, that lava is sharp! I didn't even feel this one," she murmured as she examined a long, shallow, but painful scratch all the way down her forearm. "Must have been when we were hauling ass downhill and I fell. Didn't even feel it." She disinfected her injury, opted not to bandage it, threw on her jeans and Magnum sweatshirt, and jumped back into the car.

At Volcano House, the yellow glow from the dining room looked warm and inviting after her solitary trip out of the bush. One thing K.O. loved about this area was the absence of outdoor lighting. The roads were dark, the buildings' exteriors weakly lit—moon and starlight, and Madame Pele's artwork, the only real illumination. But now, she was glad to see and smell civilization—the bustle of business, the hum of tourist chatter, and the divine odors of food from the Volcano House kitchen.

She hurried into the dining room and waved like a champion when the group cheered her. She laughed a little self-consciously and blushed as she joined them. A drink was pushed in front of her, and she didn't ask what it was, just took a big swig. Tequila Sunrise. Oh, yes.

Dinner was on the park, Melanie told them in passing, on her way from one problem to the next.

"Melanie, sit and have a bite to eat at least," K.O. urged, prompted by tequila and friendship in equal parts.

"Can't." Melanie bent down to whisper. "I don't want to bring your party down, but the action's really heating up. We're on alert right now."

"Is there any danger? I mean, like to Volcano House?"

"There's always the potential; it's a volcano." At K.O.'s expression, she added, "But not immediate, we don't think. We're closing the lower park tomorrow. Tourists are gonna be pissed." She smiled.

"Need any help?"

"Where are you scheduled tomorrow?"

"Wednesday? Back in the conference room, I think."

"I may be pulling staff from you. Can they make it up?"

"Yes. I can do maybe two or three different sessions on the same thing tomorrow, and they can catch whichever works."

"Thanks, K.O. You're great. I gotta go. First thing tomorrow, we're pulling people out of the park who have hiking and camping permits. I just hope they all went where they said they'd be, or we're gonna have a hell of a time finding them."

"What's it like on the flow?"

"Hell. Or Paradise. Gotta run." And she did.

K.O. turned back to the raucous group who hadn't seemed to hear the exchange or see their haggard boss. She didn't feel much like partying now, and after a few de-briefing questions and answers, excused herself. *Besides,* she rationalized, *they'll still talk about it, de-brief themselves, really, and be more free if I'm not there.*

She stopped at the viewing area, but saw nothing unusual. No vast pool of molten lava filled the crater below, which she had half expected.

As she crossed the parking lot, indistinct shouting drifted to her and she followed the sound to the rehearsal hall next to the art gallery.

Chagrined, K.O. realized she had forgotten all about Jerry and his production of "Deathtrap". She entered the open door and saw the actors on stage, in various pieces of costume. The set looked finished, but probably wasn't, if she remembered her theatre days correctly. Jerry sat in the first row, off to the side of an audience of empty folding chairs. He held a clipboard of yellow legal paper, filled with his bold scribble. A loose-leaf 3-ring binder lay in the seat next to him, and K.O., seating herself just behind the notebook, saw it contained the script.

"Stage right, Beth. Stage right, Beth. Stage *right!*" Jerry finally yelled to the oblivious actress. She moved an inch to the left. "Other right, Beth," Jerry said in a tone that told K.O. he'd said this many times before.

"She's a rocket scientist during the day, right?" K.O. whispered.

Jerry turned, his brows drawn down in a frown, then they immediately shot up again. "K.O.!" He hugged her awkwardly over the chair back. "You made it!"

"Yeah, but what is *it*?" K.O. nodded to Beth and the other two actors. Beth seemed to be going in circles on stage, while the other actors watched.

"Oh, God. It's been like this. She gave a great audition, but shit, she took an acting class once, and now we're paying the price." K.O. laughed. "If anyone can fix it, you can."

"I hope so," Jerry said glumly. "We open next week. Saturday is the first tech rehearsal. Sunday, we were supposed to be off. Now I don't know. Okay, you guys, take five."

The two men shuffled off the stage and, immediately pulling out smokes and lighters, went outside.

Beth stayed. "Jerry. We really need to keep working. I have some things I'd like to try with my character. I feel I need to flesh it out more." She stood, hands on cocked hips, at the edge of the stage.

"Beth, why don't you work on it, and in five minutes, I'll look at what you have, okay?"

"Well, okay, Jerry." She turned and began a combination of heavy breathing and jumping.

K.O.'s jaw dropped. "What the hell is that?" she whispered.

"I don't know. I really don't. I can't watch. Let's go out back and talk for a few. We've only been rehearsing for an hour and a half tonight, but it feels like a century."

Jerry led her to the back porch where wicker rockers faced the trees. They sat. "So, howzit going with you?"

"Pretty good. I got a little flack in the beginning—you know, *haole* coming here, taking over, whatevahs—but now it seems okay. I'm trying to make it fun while they learn something. Most of them don't have any defensive tactics training. I mean, ten years ago, maybe that was okay, but not now. This park is just waiting for something big and violent to happen." K.O. breathed in the night smell, wet, slightly sulphurous, with just a hint of the cigarette smoke wafting from the other side of the building.

"I been getting a vibe ever since I've been here." Jerry rocked slowly. "We've been rehearsing what, six weeks now? And hardly anyone's come by to see what's up, or anything. I've been in the dining room, and other than the tourists, everyone's kind of—I don't know—closed." Jerry ran a hand through his gray-streaked, sandy hair. "I've done shows here before, but something's different."

"Maybe it's this training thing. They have a lot riding on it." *On me.* "It's kind of stressful, and with the problems at the park, it just adds to it."

Jerry looked skeptical. "Someone broke in here, you know."

"No! What happened?"

"They didn't tell me the gory details, but I heard. They thought it was my actors' fault at first."

"What happened?"

"Some guy broke in and left lava on the table. And a note. But they thought it was my fault—you know, I left the doors unlocked or something. They were going to tell us we couldn't come back next season. I was so stressed when I found out."

"How did you find out?"

"The only person who's been great to us around here is the Supervisory Ranger, Melanie. She told me, like it was a big joke—no big deal—but then I heard other guys in the restaurant. One time I went there for a late dinner, and these suits were talking about how if it had been us instead of them who had left the door unlocked—they had a meeting in here that day—we would have been kicked out. Like they're looking for a reason to boot us. Pissed me off. I wanted to quit then, anyway. I thought about doing something on my own."

"Jerry! You mean like, revenge?"

"Sorta. But not really. I could never hurt a theatre. You know that, K.O. Even if it is run by assholes."

K.O. laughed. "So what are you gonna do?"

"Hang on 'til opening. Then decide. But I swear, something's changed. The same people are here that were before, so I don't know what's going on. If we make money, they'll ask us back. So, hey, tell your friends."

"Of course, I will." K.O. wondered who she could tell. She wasn't even going to be here on opening. Clayton Hsu came to mind. He knew Kamuela, who drove for a big tourist company. Maybe a word in the right ear . . . unless Clayton was mixed up in this negative-vibe thing. She didn't want to say sabotage, but what else could it be? Someone with a grudge against Jerry personally? Unlikely. She frowned.

"Whassup, girl?" Jerry hugged her neck.

"Nothing, *haole* boy." She hugged him back.

"Look who's calling the kettle white."

"You better get back to work. You're gonna have to undo all that 'fleshing out' Beth's working on."

Jerry groaned. "I know! Don't remind me. My biggest worry is that Sam and Quint will quit, too. They've been so patient, but man, I can tell they want to walk."

"Too late to replace Beth?"

"Yeah. Trouble is, when she's not so busy *acting*, she's really good. Why don't you do it? We had such good times when we worked together before."

"Yeah, I know. The best. But can't—I'm on the job here. So, you get to yours, and I'll get to mine, 'kay?"

"'Kay." They stood and hugged for a long moment.

"Off you go," K.O. gave him a little push towards the door.

"Off a cliff, more like." He pushed the screen open and K.O. heard him call the rehearsal back. As she rounded the building, she heard the high-pitched buzz, like a chain saw, of Beth's voice.

CHAPTER TWENTY

K.O. arrived at her barracks to find them in an uproar. Excited kids chattered a mile a minute and a storm of clothing swirled overhead.

"What's going on?" K.O. asked Kimmy, who dug in her backpack, pulling out a sweatshirt and watchcap.

"We're going to see the flow!" Kimmy's eyes glowed excitedly.

"What do you mean? I heard they were closing it?"

"Tomorrow. But Jane talked to her cousin, and they said if we took an escort, we could go tonight! I can't wait. I been there at night before, but not when Pele's been so active. It's awesome." Her last words were muffled as she pulled on her sweatshirt.

"Yeah? I've never seen it. What's it like?"

"Unbelievable. If you don't believe in Pele now, you sure will when you see it." Kimmy stashed two rolls of Lifesavers into her jeans' pockets. "Just in case."

"In case what?"

"Low blood sugar. Walking on the flow is hard work when you can see. It's really rough at night."

"Oh. Is it safe?"

"*You're* coming, right?"

"Where?"

"With us! To watch the flow?"

"Oh, I don't know. I have uh. . ." K.O. couldn't come up with an excuse fast enough.

Kimmy's eyes narrowed. "You're not scared are you?"

Damn right she was.

"You *have* to go. It might never be like this again. Besides, they're going to try to keep everyone out after this. I think the rangers think she's really gonna blow!" Kimmy bounced excitedly, and K.O. saw the same eagerness in all the faces in the room. Except her own, she thought.

"I guess I could," she said slowly. "What do I need?"

"Good shoes, warm clothes, a hat if you have it, flashlight, water, and a snack."

"You sound like my mother."

"Yeah, well, comes from five years of hearing Jane say it." Kimmy smiled warmly. "You'll never forget this. Even if you come again someday, you'll never forget your first night viewing. Please say yes."

K.O. remembered her first visit to Volcanoes National Park as a tourist, years ago. She had in fact, been to the park many times since then, but Kimmy was right, she reflected. She never forgot that first time, seeing the volcano building land before her eyes. She had stood on the flow, much smaller than now. It hadn't crossed Chain of Craters Road then. You could still drive all the way to Kalapana, a beautiful little coastal town, famous for its black sand beaches.

She had watched the orange river pop and bubble, becoming a waterfall, the molten heart of the earth pouring down the mountain, reaching the sea in a rush of flame and steam. She had knelt and touched the blackness with her hand, feeling the heat and pulse beneath her fingers. Tears flowing from not only the yellow mist, but something else. She was at the center of the world here. And she was nothing.

"Yes," K.O. told Kimmy firmly. "I want to come."

"Great!" Kimmy jumped up and ran to Jane. "K.O.'s going to come, too, okay? She's in our group, okay?" Kimmy ran to Angela without waiting for Jane's answer.

Jane looked over at K.O., sitting on the bunk. She laughed and nodded. K.O. smiled back.

The expedition slowly made its way to various cars, and down the long, winding Chain of Craters Road. K.O. drove Kimmy, Angela, Robert—a gangling colt, and Ehu—a small, quiet, red-headed boy. The boisterous chatter stopped as they descended from the cliff in long, steep switchbacks. The mountain fell sharply away, and K.O. was glad she couldn't see the bottom in the dark.

"There," breathed Angela. The caravan slowed at the first glimpse of orange streaks, like satin ribbons, flowing down the mountain, far ahead.

A little unnerving, but I'm okay, K.O. reassured herself. They finally reached the bottom and parked along the road. Lava had run across the road, preventing through traffic, and the park had no plans to repave until this phase of the eruption was past.

"When will that be?" K.O. had asked Melanie.

"This 'phase' has lasted years, so don't hold your breath."

Both sides of the road were lined with cars up to fifty feet from the flow. A small trailer for park personnel had been set up, and the group gathered near it.

Jane called them to attention. The fifty or so kids stood silently to hear her instructions.

"You have your groups. You each have an adult. You will stay with that adult. You will not leave your group. We are safe as long as we follow the directions, but this is a dangerous place, at a dangerous time. We are here because I convinced the park service you were well-behaved and respected me, the park, and the volcano. Prove me right. If you deviate one inch from these guidelines, you will be sent home. No questions asked, no reprieves. Understand?"

All heads nodded, even K.O.'s. As she listened to Jane, she

watched the kids. They stood stock-still, as focused as any group of police recruits, she marveled. No wiggling, no giggling, no whispering.

"Get into your groups now."

They did. Angela, Kimmy, Robert, and Ehu moved to form a squad around K.O.

"T.J. and Jody are our ranger guides here on the flow. You will listen to them, and follow behind them at all times. Not to the side, not ahead." Jane turned to the two men and nodded. "Thank you for taking us. We realize and appreciate how special this is."

T.J. and Jody began a speech similar to Jane's, and K.O.'s attention was diverted by the splash of waves against the cliff, the sizzle of lava hitting the sea, like eggs in a giant skillet, and the odd smells of brine and sulphur.

The group stepped up off the paved road onto whorls and sculptures of hardened lava, and K.O. had to watch where she put each foot. Her flashlight lit a small circle of crevices, cracks, holes and gulfs from step to step. After only a short way, her ankles told her they didn't like this one bit. She glanced up to see an army of light circles bobbing unevenly ahead of her as they picked their way farther from safety. She had been out of breath for some time when the group halted.

"We're coming to thinner lava here. A crust has formed that's safe to walk on, but stay single file, an adult with each four or five kids, behind me," Jody said. The silly facade he wore with his co-workers had been replaced by an authority in which K.O. felt safe putting her trust.

Again silently, the groups melded into a line. K.O. found herself sandwiched between Angela and Kimmy, Robert and Ehu, like bookends, with T.J. bringing up the rear.

They set off once again. The temperature under their feet had risen, and K.O. was glad to keep moving. The warm, wet air wrapped her and she felt slightly nauseated. She paused to take off her sweater, afraid to step with the fabric over her head.

"Not a good idea to stop here, K.O.," T.J. said.

As soon as she stopped, K.O. learned the reason why. The soles of her hiking boots felt as if they were melting. Sweat dripped down her breasts. She walked slowly and tied her sweatshirt arms around her waist, precariously shifting her flashlight from hand to hand to accomplish this.

The group stopped ahead. She caught up in time to hear Jody speaking of a vent they were to view. One at a time, with Jody and T.J. acting as security, they filed by a gash in the rock. When K.O.'s turn came, she froze, stunned. Just below her feet ran a flaming river. Roiling and bubbling, splashing and seething, the pace and heat of it weakened her, and she gasped, the fumes going deep into her lungs. Backing away from the fissure, she stumbled and coughed.

"K.O.! K.O.!" Taking her elbow, T.J. walked her to a pocket of comparatively fresh air. "Are you all right?"

"Yes, I think so." She coughed again and handed T.J. her flash so she could get her water bottle. "Just breathed wrong, I guess."

"Yeah, those fumes can be bad. That was something though, yeah?"

K.O. took several swallows of lukewarm water. "Yeah. Something." She drank again. "I didn't realize it would be so noisy." The crash of lava rushing through the mountain seemed to come from all sides.

"It's like the ocean sometimes. When the lava's shooting out of the top, the rocks crashing, the sounds of the mountain coming apart from inside, it's awesome."

"I bet it is."

"Are you okay to hike back now?" K.O. nodded. "I think we better get these kids back. They've been so good, but let's not beg for trouble, yeah?" He smiled, and his brown skin crinkled in the light from the vents.

T.J. gathered the group, answered a few questions, and prepared them for a different path back, one that would take them by an overground river of lava this time.

K.O. watched the group in silhouette as they passed in front of the vent. It backlit them like a campfire. *It's not a campfire, though,* she reminded herself.

On the way back to the car, she tried to forget the energy running under her feet, maybe miles, maybe inches away, but could not. She could not admit even to herself that what had made her gasp and step back from the vent was not the fumes. She had seen a smiling face with pupilless black eyes—a woman's face, framed in hair of flame, in the lava swirling under the mountain.

CHAPTER TWENTY-ONE

Melanie Ward sat in her office opposite the head geologist, a detailed topographical map of the park spread over the desk between them.

"So what you're saying Dean, is that it could blow? Is that what you're saying?"

"Activity's been increasing at a regular rate. We're seeing more and more pressure, the vents are becoming unstable. So, yeah, I guess I'm saying we could lose the lower zone." He ran a dirty hand through silvering hair.

Melanie, in uniform for eighteen hours already, slipped her shoes off and shoved them under the desk. "Okay. What are your recommendations?" She glanced out her open office door, past the dark lobby, into the black night.

"Evacuate first."

"Yeah, we're doing that. I had rangers out late this afternoon checking all the permits for locations. We'll have them out again first thing tomorrow. What else?" Melanie noted the dark circles under Dr. Welker's eyes, the ground in dirt on his hands, and his sweat-stained clothes. She knew that he, too, had been at work for at least twenty-four hours straight, along with his team, monitoring

Pele and her domain. She also noticed the excitement in those same eyes, the glowing skin under the dirt, and the taut-string energy he emanated. She knew he lived for these periods of activity, the risk, the power they displayed, and the energy he derived from them.

"We need to secure the area as best we can. You still have rangers at the Kalapana side?"

"Yes, one. Only during the day."

"You'll need one at night, too. I think this will get worse before it gets better."

Melanie flinched at the echo of her own earlier words. "Yes, I think you're right. I have personnel training all this week, with reduced staff in some areas. I already told the training officer, Katrina Ogden. Have you met her?" Negative head shake . "I told her I might be pulling people off her sessions to help."

"Okay, good." Dean pulled another set of papers over the map. "Here's the day's activity. I think we're looking at something very soon. A day or two? No way to tell. We need to be ready to evacuate everyone, if necessary."

"Everyone? You mean, like from the upper park, too?" Melanie was incredulous. "Even here?"

"Even here. I'm not sleeping, and maybe you shouldn't, either." His smile was grim. "Or maybe you should. You look terrible."

"Thanks. God. I need a vacation."

"You're living in the world's number one destination." He folded up his charts and stuffed them into his jacket.

"I feel lucky."

"I hope you do. We're going to need it. Pele's pissed about something." He pointed a dirty finger at the map of Chain of Craters Road and the East Rift Zone.

"Pu'u O'o is the likely spot. We're also monitoring some hot spots in the North East Rift Zone. I don't expect much up there, but you never know. Keep your people out of these two areas. We're no longer on a daily-report basis." He folded the map.

"We're not?"

Dean shook his head. "Hourly. I'll call you." He left the office.

Melanie stared after him, wishing she had his energy and enthusiasm, even his excitement, instead of this insistent nagging feeling that something big, irreversible, and disastrous was going to happen.

CHAPTER TWENTY-TWO

The ringing phone woke Gerald from a sound and rather painful sleep just before dawn.

"Gerald. Get up. Come pick me up. Rudy wants a meeting. He called me and says we gotta get to his house right away."

"What?"

"Dumb shit! It's Jolene. Now get your ass up and come get me! We gotta be in Rudy's office *now*!"

"'Kay den. I'm up." Gerald wasn't, but he became more so as the implication of Jolene's words reached his sleep-numbed brain. He hung up the phone in the middle of Jolene's diatribe and figured it was just as well. He'd hear it all the way to Rudy's house, anyway. Might as well hear it only once.

He rolled onto his back and glanced at the clock. 4:42 A.M. "Shit." He popped a couple of Tylenol and reached for his pants. "Gonna be a long day."

He made it to Jolene's coffee shack in record time on the deserted roads. She came out as soon as he pulled up.

"Seen my bag?" Jolene said as she hiked her short skirt up to get in the cab.

"What bag?"

"My tapestry *da kine, lolo*. Cannot find it anywhere. I hope it's not at the site."

Gerald shook his head and reversed into her dirt drive, heading to Rudy's. Uncharacteristically, Jolene was silent, which unnerved him. "So. Why does Rudy want to see us?"

Jolene picked at a nail, then chewed the cuticle. "Not sure."

"But you have some idea?" Jolene shrugged. "Is he mad about Tommy, still?" Another shrug. "The last crop was good, yeah?"

"Yeah."

"So *what*, then?" Gerald felt a roiling in his empty stomach. It spread until his hands shook on the wheel, and he grasped it tightly so Jolene wouldn't see.

"Shut up, already. You gettin' on my nerves." She didn't look at him.

He pulled into Rudy's circular drive. Ferns towered over the truck, casting eerie shadows in the security lights. He turned off the ignition and turned to Jolene as she reached for the door. He stopped her, his hand pulling on her arm.

"What aren't you telling me?"

"Stop it, Gerald. You paranoid. Let's go. He's waiting, and he knows we're here."

Gerald didn't move, but kept his hand on her arm. He squeezed it and met her gaze.

"Let go!" She jerked her arm free and jumped out, running towards the house, the passenger door open.

Gerald reached to close it, and saw in the dome's light, an unfamiliar shape poking from under the bench seat. He shut the door and pulled it out. A handbag made of flowered upholstery-like material. He left it on the floor and opened it.

A wallet, not much money. A key ring. A few cosmetics. A vial with white powder, nearly empty.

Then, what caught his eye and surprised him was a snub-nosed .38 tucked between the main compartment and the lining.

He debated keeping the gun. In the end, he tucked it into his tool-kit under his side of the bench. He took the purse with him, rolled tightly now and concealed in his hand. As he passed a bed of densely packed, brightly blooming flowers, he dropped the bag without pausing to see if the foliage concealed it and continued into the house.

Rudy and Jolene were in the study. They stopped talking when he entered.

"Sit, Gerald." Rudy waited for him. "Something's come up that we need to discuss." Rudy lit a cigar, offered one to Jolene who accepted, and one to Gerald, who did not.

Gerald rubbed his wet palms on his pants. "What's up, Rudy? The last crop was good, yeah?"

"Yes, Gerald. The last crop was fine. I was discussing something else with Jolene here, before you arrived. What kept you?"

His question surprised Gerald. "I, uh, am just real tired, you know, Rudy. We been working on the pipeline everyday, you know, to finish."

"Ah, yes. Water. Such an important part of our operation. It's a shame you've spent so much time on it. We won't have much chance to use it, I'm afraid. You'll have to spend tomorrow dismantling every piece of evidence that we—well, you, really—were ever there."

Gerald's muscles turned to water. "Take it all out?" he asked weakly. He was in good shape, athletic even, but these last days of unceasing labor in the rock had taken their toll. "Why?" he whispered.

Rudy rolled his cigar between his slender fingers, and studied him. Even at this hour, Rudy's hair was neatly combed, his pocked complexion looked as if he'd had a facial, and his clothing was casually elegant. In comparison, Gerald wore the pants he'd worn to the dig, had only cursorily washed his face and hands, and hadn't had the energy to shower last night. Gerald shifted under the scrutiny, and idly wondered if he smelled bad, and if his filthy jeans were making smudges on the watered-silk chair fabric.

"You see, Gerald. It has come to my attention that my operation at this end of the island has come under the notice of the DEA That, in fact, they are very close to closing us down. So, you and the rest of my staff will make sure nothing is left for them to find. Because if they do, arrest is the last thing you should worry about."

Gerald looked from Rudy to Jolene. They both wore similar expressions. Satisfaction, he thought. Shouldn't they be concerned? Worried? He certainly was. Rudy's words were no idle threat. Especially since Gerald knew his "partner" Jolene, was more than willing to shift loyalties with the wind, and execute him if she thought it would help her.

"You know I been working hard for you for a long time, Rudy. Sure. I'll start tomorrow. First thing."

"It is tomorrow, babooze," Jolene waved a hand at the window behind Rudy. Gray light topped with orange seeped in. "We starting now." She got up and left the room.

"Better hurry. Don't want to let Jolene get too far ahead of you, cowboy." Rudy's voice was mocking as it followed him down the corridor.

Cowboy? Why had he used that name? A nickname from another lifetime. Could he know?

Nah. Gerald got in the truck and started the engine. Jolene started on a list of things he was to obtain. How? She didn't care how. Another list of things he was to do. She didn't care when, as long as it was now.

He dropped her off at her place to change clothes. He would pick her up with the lists completed at warp speed. They would begin taking down everything today.

Halfway home, he pulled to the side of the road, engine running. He bowed his head to the wheel, and wondered if he would be alive at this time tomorrow.

CHAPTER TWENTY-THREE

After a fitful night, K.O. was wakened from a light doze by Melanie's hand on her arm. The kids were still sleeping, so she quickly got out of her canoe-shaped mattress and beckoned Melanie out the nearest door.

"What's up? You look like hell," she said, after assessing Melanie in the gray morning light.

"Change of plan. I feel like hell. Been up all night. Talking to the USGS and rangers and God knows who all. Disaster folks, everybody's on my ass."

K.O. hadn't heard Melanie sound so bleak, even when she'd first described her problems at the park.

"USGS?"

"United States Geological Survey." At K.O.'s blank look she added, "Volcano guys."

K.O. nodded her understanding. "Want some coffee?"

"Love some, but no time. Here's the deal. Today's training is revamped. I need all personnel at emergency readiness stations. They know where to go. They've hardly ever done it, but they know." She shoved a stack of papers into K.O.'s hand. "Here's the duty roster, and you're on it. I want you to help evacuate folks from the park. I've highlighted the areas in order of importance. I have you on the permit campers. God knows if they're where they're supposed to be, but do the best you can. Some you have to hike into. Are you up for that?"

K.O. felt icy fear trickle down her spine, settling at the base, making her body heavy and cold. "Sure. Anything I can do to help. What about the kids? And others up here at Volcano House?"

"No immediate danger. We don't think. We're all on alert. Desk's already called to cancel the folks who were to check in this week. Some others are opting to leave. ADA camp was supposed to go tomorrow morning, so if they want to stay, so far, that's fine. Once evacuations are complete, all non-essential personnel will leave the park. Civil Defense has already notified Hilo, and gotten the emergency warning system in place, so I think people at least *know.* Problem is, we can't really predict exactly when, where, or how bad. Could be here. Or Hilo. Or even the other side. God, we just don't know."

K.O. gently patted Melanie's hand. "Okay, just tell me what to do. I'll do it."

"Thanks. Here's a radio. Should work most places in the park, unless you get way down somewhere." She handed K.O. a two-way radio. "Regular communication's channel seven: updates, traffic, etc. Emergencies are channel three, and that's monitored twenty-four-seven. Well, everything is, now." She smiled, lips trembling. "We're all under the microscope. Any questions?"

A million. "No. I'll keep in touch. Get some food, at least. You're going to crash faster than those kids in there."

"Oh, reminds me. Pack in whatever you might need. Water, first-aid, food. I don't know how long the roads will be good, or what's going to happen. Don't take any chances. Shit!" The women grabbed each other and the door frame as an earthquake rocked the camp.

"Oh, my God!" said K.O. *Just perfect. Adds to the ambiance of the day.*

Shrieks and screams came from inside the barracks.

"Go!" she told Melanie. "I'll check inside. You're needed elsewhere. I can handle it." When Melanie hesitated, she repeated, "Go!" and plunged into chaos.

The bunks hadn't tipped, that was the first thing she noticed. Things had fallen, but that the kids had still been in bed was a blessing.

Another temblor rocked the building. More screaming. Jane and the other adults had leaped out of bed and were comforting the kids as best they could, but they looked as terrified as K.O. felt.

K.O. pulled Angela off the top bunk where she crouched, screaming, and pushed her into Kimmy's bottom bunk. She grabbed a couple more top-bunkers until they all got the idea and moved to lower berths. Gradually the screaming faded to snuffling and whimpering.

"Okay, now?" K.O. asked Kimmy and Angela, as she cuddled with them.

"No!"

"First earthquake?" she asked.

"No," said Kimmy, "but never this bad."

"Me, neither," said Angela.

"You guys going home today, then, do you think?"

"I hope not," said Kimmy.

"You hope not?"

"We need to be here," said Angela.

"It's exciting, too," added Kimmy.

"You guys are either really brave or really dumb," K.O. teased.

"Really dumb," they said, laughing.

K.O. smiled. "I'm going to check on the others for a minute." The girls held tightly to her, preventing her from rising. "It's okay, really. I'll be right back. Okay?" She gently freed herself.

The other kids were unhurt, but in various stages of fright. No more shocks came, and after a few more minutes, K.O. reached

Jane, who was hugging Ehu on the boys' side. "You guys gonna leave today?"

"I don't know yet. What do you think?" Jane peered up at her from Ehu's lower bunk, where he had wrapped himself around her, octopus-like.

"Melanie, the Supervisory Ranger, sort of deputized me, and told me they're evacuating." Jane nodded. "She also told me this area seemed relatively safe, and you're welcome to stay until tomorrow. Your last day, right?"

"Right."

"Of course, she said this before the earthquake." K.O. smiled, reassuringly, she hoped. "I'm to help with the evacuation. I think that's my training session for today. I won't be here at all. I have a map, and I'm supposed to find the permit-hikers and campers—tell them we're closed until further notice."

"I don't think we can get the kids off-island very quickly. The kids who live here, maybe we could send home. I'll call their parents and see what they want us to do. Sheesh, they live with this all the time—hanging over them." She shuddered. "I don't think I could." She absently rubbed Ehu's back.

K.O. looked sideways and saw his thumb in his mouth. He'd turned so Jane could cradle him, and he appeared to be asleep.

"Poor little guy. How old is he?"

"Ten. Kind of young for this kind of camp, but he's an old hand. Figured he could handle it. Now I'm wondering if *I* can." She gently settled Ehu back in bed and stood.

"Sorry. Just blowing off steam."

"No problem. I'd better get going. I don't know what to expect out there. Kinda nervous."

"Me, too. I'd better get going myself, and call some parents. Check blood sugars. The day waits for no man." She turned and briskly hugged K.O. "You be careful out there. If you can, let us know how it's going."

K.O. hugged her back. "Yeah. If I can."

She walked back to her end of the barracks and dressed quickly, pulling on jeans and shirt right over her flannels. She'd worn pjs ever since the first night. Now she was glad for the old-fashioned comfort they gave. She grabbed her backpack, already packed from the earlier training, and faced the girls, still in the lower bunk, but now lying side by side, holding hands, eyes wide, watching her.

"Hey. It's gonna be fine." She squatted down next to them, knees popping. Kimmy giggled. "I'm gettin' old, ladies." This time Angela smiled, too.

She put her hand on their clasped ones and gently shook them. "For luck."

"Luck," they whispered.

"Any words of wisdom for me, Angela?"

"I don't see anything."

"Is that good or bad?"

"I don't know. It's just . . . nothing."

"You girls be good. Test, eat, whatever. When I come back tonight, I should have some good stories for you about my adventures." She shook their hands again. "Okay?"

"Okay."

Angela sat up. "We won't see you tonight. Tomorrow, maybe, if we don't have to leave the park early. But anyway, not tonight."

"Okay. I see you've got your plans all made. I'll be sure to catch you up then."

Angela shook her head.

K.O. didn't know what it meant, but felt a sudden urgency to be outside, working, helping. "Gotta go." She slung the backpack over her shoulder and stepped out of the barracks into gray, leaden vog, so thick and oppressive she had to force herself not to run back inside.

"Well, Angela, you were right. I certainly can't see anything, either." K.O. licked her lips nervously and tasted mist. Metallic. Cold. Enticing.

CHAPTER TWENTY-FOUR

Driving along Crater Rim Drive towards the exit, K.O. decided to hit the closer areas first, hoping those folks nearest the volcano would already have gotten word and decamped. The earthquakes should have given them the idea.

She cautiously approached the cutoff for the first camping area and pulled in. The road, although now slightly familiar, was obscured by swirls of vog and mist, and she sweated as she looked for signs of campers. No tent, no car. She almost pulled right out again, but something told her to check more carefully.

She stepped out into the vog, and her sweat dried instantly into icy patches. She shivered. According to her map, the campers used this area in front of the car to the fire ring, but a small path led towards a viewpoint on Crater Rim Trail and on to the Research Center. She sighed and trudged off down the trail.

* * *

Farther north of K.O., Gerald and Jolene struggled to dismantle the catchment roof and piping. Fortunately, no heavy rains had filled the tank—just the regular evening showers and mist—but that was plenty as far as Gerald was concerned.

"Ai!" Gerald hissed, as a large section of corrugated metal sheeting slid suddenly from the roof, and narrowly missed slicing his leg open. His gloves seemed to afford no protection from the lava, tools, or sharp edges.

Jolene had leaned their ladder against the trees and was disconnecting the pipes. They had to remove all the materials from the area, and Gerald knew they'd make more than one load in the small pick-up. Just thinking about it made him tired.

"Hey, Jolene. I'm dropping all this sheeting here, one time, then you help me toss it in the back, 'kay?"

Jolene only grunted, and several pieces of hardware dropped from the trees.

Gerald removed the last of the metal sheets and pocketed the screws, nuts and washers.

"Jolene, how come we can't just leave this stuff here? I mean, nobody's gonna know it came from Rudy guys, yeah?"

"Rudy said to take it all. So we are. He doesn't want to leave any trace. Bum bye maybe he use this again someday, and doesn't want anyone to know someone was ever here? Think of that? No." She answered her own question, and with a shimmying of 'ohi'a branches, came down the ladder. "Okay, all that's done. We put it in the back. Come on." She picked up the light-weight piping and dragged it towards the pick-up. Gerald slowly followed with more pipe. Then they loaded the cammo netting, the sheets of roofing, and all the hardware and tools.

"Why we loading the tools, Jolene? We're just coming right back to dismantle the tank, yeah?"

"Yeah, but in the meantime, we leaving nothing." She sighed impatiently. "How many times I gotta tell you, we leaving t'ings clean, okay? Let's go." She jumped in the cab and slammed the door. Even from outside, he felt her energy buzzing like a hive of disturbed bees—angry, smoking, and barely contained.

* * *

K.O. tried to part the mist with her hands like a curtain, but the swirls just danced away. She heard almost nothing, the thick layers muffling all but the nearest rustling. *How long should I go down one blind trail?* she wondered. *I have so many places to get to, and only one day to do it. Face it. You have no idea what you're doing.* She rounded a bend and saw a small red blob. As she drew closer, the blob became a tent, with two gray shapes moving around it.

"Hello, excuse me," K.O. called.

"Hi." The shapes morphed into a middle-aged couple clad in tie-dyed shirts and Birkenstocks.

"Morning, folks. I'm Katrina Ogden, volunteering with the park service, and we need to evacuate all hikers and campers today."

The couple glanced at each other. "I told you not to smoke that thing on park property," the woman whispered to the man.

"They couldn't smell it. Now, shush." He turned to K.O., who hid a smile. "What's this about, miss?"

Miss. It had been a long while since anyone had called her miss. At some unknown point in time, she had somehow gone from a miss, to a ma'am. It made her feel old.

"An increase in the activity in the volcano has the park service evacuating all unnecessary personnel and visitors from the park." At their look of alarm, she added, "Nothing to worry about. Just a precaution. How soon can you leave?"

Melanie hadn't actually told her to escort people out, but she thought she should at least wait until they were on their way.

"I don't know. Half hour?" The man looked at the woman.

"If those earthquakes were what this is about, I'm leaving *now!*"

"Did you folks drive or pack in?"

"We drove. The car's over there." The man waved vaguely in the direction of the main camping area, where K.O. had seen no car.

"Well, let's get you out of here." She turned to find the woman had already taken down the tent, and was stuffing it into a remarkably tiny nylon bag. The man threw some cooking utensils into a backpack, and rolled up the two thin, rubber sleeping mats. Sleeping bags, already rolled, sat near the fire ring. K.O. doused the fire, spread the coals with her boot, doused them again, and sprinkled dirt. While she did this, the couple hoisted large, top-heavy packs on their backs, and started marching down the trail.

"Okay, uh, see you," K.O. called. She shook her head. The couple waved without turning. K.O. followed, back to her car, where the couple continued across the lot to another trail, and disappeared.

The car seemed warm and comforting after the icy, insubstantial walls of vog. She pulled the map to her, determined her next stop, and started the engine.

* * *

Gerald drove down Highway 11 to the vacant lot behind Rudy's property to dump the supplies. Vacant *lot* was a misnomer really, since other than Rudy's elaborate fence, no property lines were visible. If property stakes had ever been set, the jungle had swallowed them long ago.

"Turn here," Jolene said, sharply and unnecessarily. Gerald had been to this dumping ground before. So had others, from the display of derelict cars, a washing machine with no door, bags of refuse, and a roll of carpet—the more recognizable items amid the decaying rot in the humid rainforest. Although this spot was close to Rudy's property, he told Gerald not to worry about it, since so many others used it as well. If no one stole the pieces, they could be recovered later and rebuilt at a new location.

Gerald and Jolene quickly hauled the materials off the back of the truck and left them where they fell. The ground here was smooth and wet, easy to walk and drive on. The lush ferns and

towering growth felt confining after the openness of the volcano.
The vog was sure something this morning. *Haven't seen it like
this in a while,* Gerald mused, as they began the drive back to the
site.

"You think we can break that tank down and get it out in one
trip?" Gerald asked Jolene.

"Maybe." She was obviously thinking of something else. She
shifted her body to look at him as she spoke. "We get that tank
out and the first fifty feet or so of line going to the caves. Then we
drive closer to the caves, and take out da stuff from there. What
you t'ink?"

Gerald was surprised at her asking for his opinion about
anything besides the actual growing process. "Sounds good. I'm
getting hungry. When do we eat?" She seemed pleased that he
deferred to her. He planned to keep it that way.

"How about after we do the tank? It's still real early. Breakfast
after the tank, then we can work on the pipe. That gon' take a
while, there's so much of it."

He remembered how much of it there was. He had laid it all.
The only easy part had been going under Highway 11. He had
used an existing but out of service drainage pipe. Filled with weeds,
debris, and rat carcasses, the cement tunnel, although relatively
easy to use, was disgusting. He'd rather lie belly down in the *a'a*
and chisel down a foot than go through the tunnel again. Maybe,
he wouldn't have to. He could just pull out the pipe from one
end—he hoped. He shivered at the thought of slogging through
the extra-long conduit.

"What?" Jolene asked.

"What?"

"You shaking or something? What?" She sounded more irritated
than concerned. He figured she didn't want him to get sick and
have to do the work herself.

"Nothing. Just a chill."

"Roll up your window then, stupe." She turned and looked

out her own. Rather than explain, he rolled the window up.

They pulled into the too-familiar clearing. With only the occasional curse or direction from Jolene, they began to dismantle the tank. She had concealed it behind a rise of existing lava, adding more stones and dead tree limbs to blend in. Removing the facade was relatively simple. Unscrewing the many bolts and controlling the unwieldy panels, less so. After only a few minutes, the cordless drill gave out.

"Didn't you recharge the battery?" Jolene asked.

"Yes." But he really couldn't remember. He'd been so tired.

"Yeah, I bet. Breakfas' gonna be late. I hope you happy."

They were reduced to using pliers, screwdrivers, whatever would fit the mismatched hardware. Jolene flipped a screwdriver end over end in her hand, eyeing him. He pretended not to notice, but moved to the backside of the tank. In a moment, the slap, slap of the tool was replaced by the motion of the tank as she unfastened a panel.

As they neared the halfway point, a jarring earthquake felled them onto the sharp rubble. They cowered beneath the leaning tank sides. Jolene's piercing screams could be heard for miles, Gerald was sure. He crawled quickly and painfully to her and slapped his hand over her mouth. Her eyes were huge and round, and she forced air through her nose with a whistling sound that Gerald would have found funny, were he not just as petrified.

"Ssshhh. Ssshhh. Someone gonna hear." She continued to whimper, frozen, eyes locked on his, her hands clasped over his fingers on her mouth, as if to keep in her terror. He pulled her to his chest and rocked her, even as the earth rocked them again, sending shivers up the sides of the unsecured tank. Gerald felt more than saw a wood and metal panel fold above him like origami, and collapse. As its shadow arced down, he dragged Jolene and twisted, pushing her under him as the tank erupted like a blooming flower. Gallons of stagnant water poured over them in a fetid waterfall, and an ominous crunch finished the ballet as a panel crashed into his curved back, knocking the wind out of him and crushing Jolene onto the resisting spikes of lava. Her whimpers turned to moans, his own joining in as he tried to push the panel off.

His back felt dislodged, disconnected somehow, but he managed to push off the piece and roll away from Jolene. She lay immobile, but finally silent. When no more shocks came, he gradually pushed to all fours. His back hurt, but he stood at last with an audible grinding of bone. Jolene had not moved, but her eyes were open.

"Jolene? Jolene." He moved her arms and legs, and decided they weren't broken. He pulled her to a sitting position. Her left arm, the one crushed against the rollicking earth, was in ribbons. Bands of skin and blood, festive as July fourth, trickled down her arm. Her lower body had been better protected by her jeans.

He ran limping to the truck and grabbed a water bottle and a warm can of Hawaiian Sun juice. At her side, he opened the juice and held it to her lips.

"Drink this. Good for shock." She turned her head away at first, then drank, tentatively at first, then greedily.

While she drank, he gently took her arm and rotated it away from her body. He poured water on her wounds, and a pink stream followed the drops of bright blood, trickling like tears onto the crevices and disappearing. She seemed not to notice. He was relieved to see that the scrapes, although they had removed a great deal of skin, were not deep. The bleeding had already stopped. He used his filthy T-shirt, cleaner on the inside, to blot the blood and water. He looked up to see her watching him.

"T'anks, eh?"

"Yeah. No problem. It's not bad. Hurt much?"

"Nah. Earthquake was worse, man. I hate those t'ings." She struggled to stand.

"Maybe you should rest a little more before we go back. You have first-aid stuff at the house, yeah? Or we could stop at a store."

"Go back? We not going back. We gotta do this tank *today.*

Then we gotta drive down, and get the cave started. No time for dis shit."

Gerald felt his mouth go slack. "We almost died! That tank could have killed us, one noddah inch!"

"Rudy don't care. No excuses. I'd rather face another earthquake than Rudy piss off at me."

Her dark skin was gray and pasty. From the shock or thoughts of Rudy's retribution, Gerald could not tell. "Okay. We go." Gerald found his screwdriver, dropped in a crack, and turned back to the tank.

"This makes it real hard, now, Rudy. You know that," Gerald heard Jolene mumble. "I no like do dis no more. Da las' time. For sure. Da las' time."

As he pulled off a warped and shrieking panel, from the other side of the tank he thought he heard Jolene crying.

CHAPTER TWENTY-FIVE

K.O. checked two more sites thoroughly, finding the campers had already gone. She had one site left in the upper park, and would then move on to the lower park, closer to the flow. She was torn between the excitement of seeing land created and witnessing awesome power, and the fear of more earthquakes opening up the ground under her.

She followed her map and found the road that led to the area where she had taught rescues. It seemed easier to find in daylight, although it was still gloomy and gray. She didn't remember any signs of hikers or campers when they had done their breakneck charge down the wash. Wouldn't she have seen a tent or something? Maybe not in their rush.

The flash of white she'd seen. Maybe that wasn't just a juice can, as she'd thought. But that was farther down, where she'd made the wrong turn before. She could be misreading the map. Maybe she was one site too far over? She began to second guess herself, filled with doubt. She didn't want to miss anyone out here. It was dangerous, and becoming more so. Visions of a torrent of lava ripping through some family's campsite spurred her to explore the next trail, trying to find where she imagined the flash to be a helpless group of nature-lovers.

She had worked up a good head of steam, bordering on panic, when she finally found the area she sought. It was anti-climactic to find no one there. Not even a juice can this time. Remembering the first couple, she continued on foot down the wash, carefully checking for signs of campers, helpless or otherwise.

Her ankles continued to protest until she decided to give up. Near noon, hungry and tired, she sat on a jumble of rock to rest before heading back to her car, and onto the lower park. *Rats!* In her hurry to rescue her campers, she'd taken off down the wash without her backpack. No food, water, or first-aid kit, she thought ruefully. *Glad none of my students are here to witness this.* She pushed off and stood, stretching her aching muscles, arms overhead. She rolled her neck and saw rusty smudges on her upraised hands. Blood?

She glanced around for the carcass or entrails of whatever had been killed and eaten here. Nothing. No trail of blood either. Weird. Just drops on the rocks, nearly invisible on the dark surface, but upon closer examination, the drops had thickened to a sticky film, as though whatever had bled there had remained for some time.

She looked around the clearing uneasily now, unsure. Keeping one eye on the surrounding trees, she carefully checked the area around the blood. No footprints, of course, but she did find something that surprised her. The back side of the pile of tumbled lava had been dug out. Something circular had left an imprint in the haphazard rock. Something hidden.

Unable to hypothesize further, she continued around the rubble, and stopped when a metallic flash caught her eye. A Japanese *go-yen* gleamed in the low light. A five yen coin. Brassy in color, beautiful in design, *go-yen* were often used for jewelry because the hole in the center of the coin made it ideal for earrings, bracelet charms, or necklaces, and the coins were said to bring the wearer good luck. *Nothing unusual in that.* Odd to find it here, but one of her team could have lost it during the training.

It hung from a black silk thong and had an unusual symbol engraved over the coin's markings. Hadn't she'd seen one like it recently? But where?

She tucked it into her pocket and hurried back to her car. The day was passing quickly and she still had the lower park to check. She reviewed her map and chugged a whole bottle of water.

As she drove, she fingered the *go-yen,* trying to remember who she'd seen wearing one on a similar cord. She hoped it would bring her luck today. She would need it.

* * *

Gerald and Jolene dumped the tank parts, and headed to Jolene's house for breakfast and a change of clothes. They had intended to eat at Kitty's Diner in Volcano, but feared her injuries would make them conspicuous.

While Jolene showered and cleaned her cuts, Gerald fried Portuguese sausage, eggs and rice.

"Hey, where's the shoyu?" he called from her kitchenette.

"In the cabinet," came a faint reply.

Separated from the rest of the living room by a Formica-topped counter, the cooking area was barely big enough for one person, and *then* only if you didn't turn around much. Jolene had informed him that she was going to clean up, and that if he wanted something to eat, he'd better cook it.

He'd rummaged for the three staples in every Hawaiian house besides Spam and Hawaiian Sun juice.

He finished frying the rice with soy sauce and scooped it onto plates, as Jolene appeared in the bathroom doorway. Paler, but clean and bandaged, she sat at the plastic dinette table. Gerald set the food in front of her, and she turned her head away.

"I don't think I can eat."

"You gotta eat. You gon' faint if you don't eat, and we have to do the cave, too, yeah?"

Jolene sighed, nodded, and picked up her fork. She took a tiny bit of rice, a bite of sausage, and a lump of egg, and chewed.

"Got any coffee?" Gerald asked, after watching this excruciatingly slow portioning process for several bites.

"Freezer."

"Want some?"

"Yeah. Gerald?" She put down her fork.

"What?" He measured coffee and water, and punched the on button.

"You ever think about quitting? Just leaving?"

He stared at her, unwilling to speak. This sounded an awful lot like Tommy's last words.

"Not really."

"But sometimes? You do, right?" She nodded to herself and picked up her fork again. "You do." It was a statement.

Gerald ate quickly, nervously. He didn't want to, but knew he needed fuel, too, for what he had to do. "Let's go. Couple hours to do the pipes, then we got da cave. Why don't we jus' do da cave first? Isn't that more important? We can do the pipes laters, yeah?"

Jolene's jaw worked as she finished her food, then swallowed her coffee. She finally looked at him. "Jus' do your job, man. It'll all be over soon. We go."

CHAPTER TWENTY-SIX

Gerald parked the pick-up on an access trail, half a mile from the tank site. He and Jolene wore leather gloves and tossed rocks aside, unburying literally a half-mile of pipe. They had not needed to secure it to the ground, other than weighting it with rocks. They each carried a hacksaw and severed the PVC near the cemented joints.

The labor was backbreaking and intense. Every ten poles or so, one of them would gather the pipes and drag them back to the truck. Periodically, Gerald moved the truck down the mountain. Finally, they reached the tree line north of Highway 11 and took a break.

Gerald sat at the base of a tree and leaned his head back, breathing heavily. Black spots danced in front of his eyes. He drank slowly but steadily from first one, then a second water bottle. His hands shook as they draped over his bent knees.

Jolene didn't look any better than he felt. Her eyes were glazed and her face flushed, with a ring of paler skin around her mouth. Her hands lay slack in her lap, legs outstretched.

Gerald estimated that they had walked at least five miles, dismantling the mile of pipeline, hauling loads to the truck. He had thought to pull the pipe from the tunnel under the road, then dump the load before continuing on to the cave site.

Now he wasn't so sure. His body, in good shape from hiking around the mountain, and the physical exertion of his job, had been tested to the limit the past few days. When he tried to get up, his legs didn't respond. He pulled a squashed Milky Way candy bar from his pocket and offered it to Jolene, who shook her head.

With shaking hands, he unwrapped the candy and ate it in two bites. He fished a second out of the other pocket. This one was even more squished, and he had to lick the candy off the inside wrapper. His jaw cramped with the sweet, sticky sensation, and saliva flooded his mouth. He felt the sugar filling him up, like fuel in a gas tank.

He sat unmoving for five more minutes, then turned to Jolene. "I am not doing this tunnel pipe right now. I'm too tired. I want to drive the load we have and dump it. Then eat again. I can't do this right now." He was arguing, but Jolene had said nothing. He watched her empty face until she looked at him. She nodded slowly. He helped her up, and like an elderly couple, they shuffled towards the truck, hidden in the trees, away from the road.

The sound of an approaching car made them hesitate, staying concealed. Gerald watched as a blue Geo Metro drove slowly down the misty highway, its single occupant leaning towards the windshield, straining to see. The chocolate churned in his stomach and he felt nauseated. The blue blob disappeared into the mist, but a flashing orange light told him it had turned into the park.

The fear of something unknown, combined with his physical discomfort, made him hustle Jolene to the truck and quickly leave the area.

* * *

K.O. had washed the blood off her hand, but it still felt sticky. She drove cautiously, crossing Highway 11 in the thickening mist.

She squinted and proceeded down Chain of Craters Road to a turn-off leading to Napau Trail. A campsite was supposed to be along there somewhere. The little triangle on her map that meant "tent camping" was far along the trail, and ominously close to Pu'u O'o vent, the previous focus of volcanic activity, still active but of less immediate concern.

Near Pu'u O'o, a new vent had opened, Kupaianaha, which had the U.S. Geologic Service, HVNP, and the community of Kalapana in an uproar.

According to Melanie, Pu'u O'o's cinder cone had maxed out at 900 feet high, and was no longer able to vent the massive amounts of lava Pele felt compelled to birth. The pressure had been too much, and the new vent had ripped open, spewing 600,000 cubic yards of roiling lava a day, in a one to three mile span, sometimes 100 feet deep. The immediate concern was not only for the park, but for the subdivisions of Royal Gardens, Kapa'au, and Kalapana Gardens, containing approximately 140 homes and numerous businesses.

The community had been urged to evacuate, but was resisting. Some local families who had been in the area for several generations, and a newer *haole* population begun in the 1960s, were reluctant to abandon their homes and belongings, but more importantly, their sense of community.

K.O. pulled off and parked, this time remembering to hoist her backpack onto her tired shoulders.

Thirty minutes later, mist swirling densely about her, she knew she was lost. The tumbled lava beneath her feet looked just like the lava to either side. She had not seen the rock-cairn trail markers for some time, but had put that down to the mist.

A glimpse of sun, that's all she'd need to tell her direction. She knew if she headed south, she'd end up back towards the flow eventually. Not that she wanted to be near the flow, but then, at least she'd know where she was.

She trudged ahead. Going back wouldn't get her anywhere—

she could be walking in a big circle, for all she knew. The land rose ahead of her; a sparse tree line came into view. A fallen *'ohi'a* provided a seat as she gasped, out of breath, and groped for a water bottle. The mist seemed thinner here, although the air had a metallic tang that made her throat ache.

Her isolation felt permanent, somehow. It would be hours before anyone thought to look for her, even if the park found the manpower for a search.

Great. I'm here to help, and I'm gonna need rescuing.

That thought was enough to make her stand up. The humiliation of rescuing the training officer was too much to contemplate. And what about those campers? It was unthinkable that they would still be out here, in these conditions, but really, people could be stupid.

She was reminded of a call to a car break-in at the Pearl Ridge Shopping Center parking structure back on O'ahu. She'd been taking the police report of damages and items stolen, when she noticed the traffic in that section of the garage was suddenly heavier. She was already hot and cranky in the humid, open-air garage, standing uncomfortably on the sloping cement ramps while she listened to the litany of the tourist who had rented the car.

"Didn't they tell you not to leave your belongings in the rental?" she asked.

"Well, sure. But this is Hawai'i. It's supposed to be safe. Otherwise, how you gonna keep the tourists coming back?" The man in his loud Aloha shirt was sure it was some "young punks,'"and vowed to press charges. K.O. told him he'd never see his stuff again, but he didn't listen. As the stream of cars slowed, she saw they were all going the wrong way in the one-way aisle. Following the tail car was a security Cushman, driven by an elderly, pot-bellied guard K.O. knew well.

"Hey, Clarence. What's up?" She gestured to the cars proceeding the wrong way, at two miles an hour.

Clarence glumly shook his head. "One goes the wrong way.

The others follow. People are like sheep. They are like that." He waved and slowly followed the caravan around a cement pillar.

K.O.'s mood had lifted.

She smiled now, remembering Clarence and his morose comment about sheep.

She imagined a bunch of campers sitting around, roasting marshmallows in the flames from the lava. She shook her head. Maybe they didn't need to be rescued, but it was her job to check, and she was going to do her job.

Somewhat renewed, but increasingly skeptical, K.O. once more set off.

* * *

Down on the lava shield, the geologists and Melanie watched a fissure in the mountain. Each held a shield for protection from the 2000-degree spatter that shot well over their heads. They looked like police officers in riot gear.

They measured temperatures and took samples, comparing the flow from moment to moment.

"This is like a river, now," Melanie commented.

"The glacier part is over, now we're into rapids," said Dean, the head geologist.

"It's sure something to see." Melanie felt as if she were melting, and shifted her feet back and forth to reduce the heat. "What's happening with Kalapana? Civil Defense is monitoring, but it looks bad."

"The flow is so fast at this point, we're telling people to get out, but you know how it is. 'Madame Pele won't take my house.' Yeah, right."

They all jumped back as a huge spray of lava shot out of the slit and cascaded where a geologist had been standing moments before.

"You okay, Brad?" Dean called, his voice hoarse over the roar.

Brad nodded and moved back a few more feet, adjusting his

shield. The lava surged out for several moments before it settled into a pattern of smaller spouts.

"Royal Gardens is threatened now, and Kapaʻau. Nothing we can do," said Dean.

"What do you want from us?"

"Keep everybody out until this stabilizes."

"Okay. Keep in touch. I'm going back up top to see how the evacuation's going. Got people out here, still." She thrust a six-pack of water at him.

"Thanks."

"Be careful." His attention was already back on his staff.

Melanie picked her way over the steaming crust of lava, watching for hot spots. A skylight—a small hole—a foot in diameter was on her left, and she paused to watch the raging flow. She loved it here, but it scared her sometimes. She shivered and carefully continued onto older, cooler lava, finally breathing comfortably when she could see the trailer on Chain of Craters Road. She looked back at the black mountain streaked with orange flame, terrifying and wonderful.

She glanced at her watch. It had taken her an hour to make the check on the team on the flow. Radios didn't work this far down. She dreaded the next check, which would come after dark.

CHAPTER TWENTY-SEVEN

The afternoon was passing quickly, and K.O. felt no closer to the campsite she sought than she had an hour ago. At one point the mist parted, opening a beautiful vista. She stood on a slight rise, mid-way down the mountain. The cobalt blue sea, a shimmering silken cape at the cliff's base, reflected mountain, clouds, and lava. A plume of steam several hundred feet high rose below her. She saw Chain of Craters Road, black pavement matching the surrounding black lava, but smooth and soft-looking. To her left, the lava shield. Now that she was above, it was even more terrifying. Pu'u O'o vent, still active, boiled and seethed, but since the opening of the second vent, no longer displayed the projectile fire show.

Kupaianaha was a different matter. Larger than she'd imagined, the shield covered the area as far as she could see. Kupaianaha meant strange, wonderful, extraordinary. It was that and more. K.O. stood frozen, fear and awe rushing through her. She felt it in her blood, along her veins and arteries, tingling in her scalp and fingertips, excitement in her belly. Here, the mist was gone, but the ash and vog continued to spiral up and away, giving her this gift.

Like sparrow to cobra, she was compelled to watch the fountains, the rivers, the cascades of lava as they plunged towards the sea.

The rivalry between Pele and her sister, the goddess of the sea *Na maka o Kaha'i*, was never clearer than standing here, watching the battle. Pele the destroyer.

Acres of forest, home to birds, animals, plants, all paved over in this rush of molten rock. Now, people's homes were endangered. How much would be erased before it stopped? If it stopped. Again, K.O. felt the stirrings of humility, of a power greater than humanity, controlling the outcome. No wonder they prayed to Pele here, for indeed, man had no say in this place.

But K.O. also saw the hundreds of acres Pele had added to the Big Island, birthing land and life from her fertile spirit, sending it rushing to be doused in her sister. Pele the creator.

K.O. tore her eyes from the hypnotic plumes then widened them in horror as she spied small figures below on the shield. She saw them dance back as spray erupted from a slit in the rock. Merely dots on the volcano, they faced death in the quest for knowledge. As she watched, she grew calmer, seeing that the people indeed knew their limits, as best they could in an unpredictable landscape. She pulled out of her paralysis and shook her head.

"Ouch." Her foot had fallen asleep, and she gingerly rotated it, carefully testing it with her weight to regain the feeling. "What the hell was that?" she wondered at her disconnected thoughts. She turned away from the view and saw the brown sign with white lettering denoting a camping area. "Duh."

She performed a cursory check and found no signs of recent camping. The fire ring was long dead, no rubbish, no sign of humanity. Now, to find the trail. No apparent trail. "Crap." She might as well have flown here, for all the clues there were to the trail.

The easiest opening led to the lava shield. "I don't think so." So she climbed up again, through thinning *'ohi'a,* broken boulders, and clearer air. Over the rise, the forest grew denser, and she picked her way into the growth.

"This is why I was never a Girl Scout," she grumbled as she stepped over logs and through brush. "Or maybe if I had been," she panted, "I would know where the hell I was, and what I was doing. Oh, man!" K.O. faced a blank wall. Lava piled, mounded, twenty feet straight up. No question of climbing it. She stood panting at the face of the rise, numb with frustration.

"Nothing left to do, I guess." A headache was forming behind her eyes and she pressed the palms of her hands against them to drive it away. She sat and pawed through the pack until she found an energy bar and a juice box. She forced herself to eat slowly, putting the wrappers and box back into the pack—even the annoying scrap of cellophane on the straw. She drank a bottle of water.

The area sloped slightly, and she decided to follow the cliff down—easier that way. She rose reluctantly and stretched, testing her legs. A little jelly-like, but not bad. At least she had completed her mission. Assuming she ever found her way out of here, and back to park headquarters, she could help out somewhere else. The sudden thought, of an actual chair and flush toilets, cheered her enough to spur her on.

The sky grew darker and grayer, and K.O. paused, stepping east towards the lava shield to check the eruption. It was harder to see, but it didn't look any different. Her watch told her it was getting dark because the day was ending.

A little bubble of panic rose at the thought of being stuck here after dark. She returned to the cliff, determined to follow its southwesterly course. The rise grew less severe, more rounded, and she paused to get her bearings. She heard voices.

No. That couldn't be right. Out here in—*where?*

The campers. It must be them. Maybe they were lost like she was. *Great.* How could she help them when she didn't know where she was? If they were hurt, she had first-aid, water, energy bars.

She listened carefully.

The voices, rising and falling, came from the other side of the mound. She rounded the lower end, remembering the upper end became the sheer cliff, but found no people. The voices stopped and started as she walked. She couldn't tell where they came from and was about to call out when she saw an opening in the mound—a dark slit, just large enough for a person to pass through. She leaned close to listen. The voices were indeed coming from inside the mound.

"I gotta do this. Tol' me to take care of you, so I am."

"No! You crazy! I can help. Don't do this."

"You double-crossing us, man. You're a cop, and you been talking too much."

"Yeah, maybe I *was* a cop. But I been dirty too long. Check it out! I was straight with you."

"If you was straight with us, you'd a tol' us you was a dirty cop. If *that's* even true. You put the whole operation in trouble. Look at the crops we lost 'cause a you!"

"Me? I only been helping! You treat me like one slave, and I do everyt'ing you say." A pause. "Sure. You guys believe me, then, yeah?"

"Not."

"Don't shoot. You don't have to do this. I just leave, okay?"

"No. You talk too much, too unreliable, too soft."

K.O. stood frozen outside the cave. She felt for her weapon, and found her ankle bare. She remembered she had decided she wouldn't need it; it would just be heavy and cumbersome on a rescue. *Stupid.*

What to do? Charge into a dark cave with no weapon? Not a good idea.

As these thoughts ran through her head, she heard a scuffling sound and a thump, followed by a gunshot.

CHAPTER TWENTY-EIGHT

Gerald knew his exhausted body wasn't working quite right. He and Jolene had dumped the pipe, and continued down the line to the cave. Upon arrival, he was stunned to see that all the marijuana plants were gone.

"What happened? Someone found our stash!"

"Nah. I cleared 'em out. Save us time, now."

"When did you have time to do that? We've been working for two days on the upper end of the project."

Jolene ignored him. She continued to dump dirt from the beds, leaving it on the cave floor, and dragged the beds out of the large, well-hidden, north end of the lava tube. The south opening was much smaller, and they rarely used it.

Gerald had grown increasingly uncomfortable with Jolene's behavior. In his mind, she had always been strange, but since Tommy's murder, he thought her stability had deteriorated. He figured she was smoking the product they grew, and knew from the contents of her purse that she was also using something stronger. He assumed that Rudy trafficked in other drugs, but he'd never been able to find out for sure. Jolene and Rudy both were very closed-mouthed about the operation, despite his year-long efforts to win their trust.

Today, especially, Jolene seemed distracted—exhausted one minute, giddy and hyper, eyes over-bright the next. The closer they'd come to the cave, the more agitated and jumpy she'd become. Gerald had put it down to the anxiety of discovery, but now he wasn't so sure. Her vague explanation for the pot crop seemed strange, given that they'd just put the watering system in. She must have started removing the plants just after his last assessment, like she knew they wouldn't be using the cave. But how could she know? Unless Rudy had told her to clear out and not tell him. That made sense. Jolene didn't sneeze without Rudy's permission.

But why would they clear out the cave, then make it seem like a recent decision? He groaned inwardly at the memory of his intense labor, laying pipe for Rudy and his company, and all for nothing. Anger surged through him and he stepped up to Jolene as she pulled down extension cords and piled up Gro-lights.

"So, Rudy told you to clear this out, yeah?" She ignored him. "And you jus' let me work my ass off, diggin' in the lava for nothing? Right?" Jolene stepped around him. He pushed her shoulder, forcing her back. "Answer me!"

"I was out there, too, you know."

"Sure. So what's really going on here? You know something, and I got the feeling I'm going to pay the price."

She looked steadily at him, her pupils large and black in the semi-dark. "Go put these in the truck." She indicated the piled equipment. The walls were bare, the floor littered with dirt from the beds, but all signs of the pot-growing had melted away.

"No. Tell me what's going on."

"Go put the stuff in the truck," she repeated.

He didn't move. His fists balled at his sides, anger boiled, and he forced himself not to hit her smug face. He smelled his own sweat, musky and heavy, and tinged with fear. He was afraid, and didn't know why.

"I'll tell you when you get back. Go put the stuff in the truck."

Her features were part in shadow, and her slow breathing seemed loud in the cave, a longer rhythm against his own ragged breaths. He held her gaze a moment longer, then did as she said. *Again.* But for the last time, he swore to himself.

When he returned, filthy and out of patience, it was nearly dark. He found Jolene standing in the southern cave, unmoving. "So, now. Tell me. What the hell's going on?" He took a pace towards her. She faced him. She held a small gun, barely visible in the gray light from the cave slit. He froze. "Jolene! What you doing?"

"I gotta do this. Rudy tol' me to take care of you, so I am."

"No! You crazy! I can help. Don't do this."

"You double-crossing us, man. You're a cop, and you been talking too much."

Gerald swallowed. How much did they know? That he was a Hilo police officer, nearing suspension, committing nearly every illegal act on the books, was not a secret. He had worked hard to achieve that reputation. Things were not supposed to go this way.

Like Tommy. Although Gerald had tried to remove his friend's body from the field, he had failed. The feral dogs and pigs, along with myriad insects, had succeeded where he had not. Now he wondered what Rudy had really had on Tommy, who had been with the operation longer than he. In fact, Tommy had brought him in. When Tommy was killed, Gerald had hidden his fear, unable even to tell anyone about his death. He'd had no one to talk to since then, and it was driving him crazy. Gerald forced his words out. He had to walk carefully here. "Yeah, you know I *was* a cop. But I been dirty too long. Check it out. I was straight with you." Jolene's face was nearly invisible in the darkness of the cave. The northern end was in complete darkness, the southern slit a pale orange glow, part sunset, part eruption.

Jolene's back was to the slit, and in silhouette she waved the small gun casually as she spoke. "If you was straight with us, you'd a tol' us you was a dirty cop. If that's even true. You put the whole operation in trouble. Look at the crops we lost 'cause a you!"

"Me? I only been helping! You treat me like one slave, and I do everyt'ing you say!" He felt for the gun he'd taken from Jolene's bag, and had kept with him ever since. "You guys believe me then, yeah?"

"Not." He felt more than saw her level the weapon, confirming her decision to shoot.

"Don't shoot! You don't have to do this. I just leave, okay?" He wasn't sure he could avoid a bullet in these close quarters. He also didn't think he'd have the time or visibility to pull his own weapon and shoot her in the dark.

"No. You talk too much, too unreliable, too soft."

Gerald knew he was out of time. He lunged sideways and down, crashing her against the wall with him. He felt the bullet tear into his upper arm, but the pain he expected didn't come. What did come was the force of the shot flinging him off Jolene and pushing him, stumbling, falling out the slit.

The air outside was comparatively cool, and the light brighter than inside. He zigzagged away from the slit, downhill, towards a tumble of sloping rock. As he ran, ankles screaming, bones twisting, he felt for the gun in his waistband and yanked it out.

Jolene screeched and hurtled out of the cave after him, as he figured she would. As he ducked behind the pile of rock, he hit his left side and the pain felled him. His eyes saw stars blacker than the approaching night, and he collapsed to his knees, the blood streaming freely down his arm. Through the haze, he knew he had to keep the gun. He was dead without it. He prayed he'd made it to the pile before Jolene had seen him in the dusk.

The dizziness dissipated and he cautiously looked towards the cave. What he saw astonished him. Jolene stood at the mouth of the slit, gun in hand, head swiveling, hair flying in a darker halo, the bright flowers on her shirt a beacon. Next to her, around the side of the entrance, was another woman. Unsure of feature or dress, but nevertheless he could tell it was a woman.

Was he hallucinating? Had Pele come to save him? He knew Pele appeared in many guises to both aid and warn. What was her mission now? He shook his head and squinted again, but the woman had vanished. Her appearance gave him hope and strength, and he turned and ran in the only direction he could. Pele had shown him the way. To Kupaianaha. To the volcano.

CHAPTER TWENTY-NINE

Melanie finished a check of the upper park prior to making her first night check of the flow team. All was as it should be—radio checks intact, staff at appropriate posts—until she reached the barracks and spoke to Jane, the American Diabetes Association camp coordinator.

"Jane, do you mean K.O. hasn't been here since early this morning?"

"I haven't seen her. And she did promise the girls she'd see them when she returned." She nodded to Angela and Kimmy, packing slowly, but obviously listening at their nearby bunks.

Melanie took Jane's elbow and turned her away from the girls. "So, you saw her at what, eight? And she said she'd check the campsites on the map I'd given her, right?" Jane nodded. "Please don't let anything have happened to the police liaison," she muttered. At Jane's startled look, she added, "I'm sure she's fine. I just have a lot on my mind. It's possible she found some people who needed help and is out of radio range. Hell, maybe she's having dinner right now." She smiled and ran a hand through hair that had been ruffled so many times that day.

"If she comes back here, want me to call you?" Jane asked.

"I have another check to do on the shield, and it puts me out of radio range. It'll take me at least a couple of hours to get back here. Call this number." She scribbled on a wrinkled napkin. "This is emergency, only. Don't call it just to check. Call it if she comes back."

"Okay," said Jane softly, pocketing the scrap.

"*When* she comes back." Melanie took Jane's hand. "Thanks. If you haven't heard by the time I get back, I'll have to start looking for her." She turned to leave. "But I don't know *who's* gonna look," she mumbled, pushing outside into the night.

Inside the barracks, Jane turned to the girls. "Everything's fine."

"No, it's not," Angela said.

"Well, no," admitted Jane. "But K.O. is a trained officer. She'll be fine. She can take care of herself."

"I know," said Kimmy.

"She won't have to," said Angela at the same time. Jane didn't hear. She had turned back to encourage the other campers to pack everything except what they'd need first thing in the morning.

* * *

Melanie drove rapidly down the familiar Chain of Craters Road. She willed the twenty-mile drive to pass quickly. She knew she was speeding, but didn't care.

She had to get to the trailer and see if anyone had heard from K.O. Then she had to hike, in the dark, to the active flow and make the appointed check with the geologists. She had a duty to K.O., but she also had a duty to the whole park, maybe the whole state.

Her operation was under a microscope, now that the eruption was getting worldwide media coverage. She'd heard stories both live and on the radio all day of her staff pulling idiot reporters and camera folks, not to mention tourists traipsing in from the sparsely staffed Kalapana side, out of dangerous areas. So far, no one had been injured, but it was only a matter of time, she thought glumly. The weight of it all bowed her shoulders and dampened her confidence.

At last she reached the trailer parked where the flow had crossed the road. From here, it was all on foot. She dashed to the trailer, but no one was inside. She quickly checked the radio log, the daily log of visitors, the accident and incident logs. Nothing indicated K.O. had been hurt, seen, or even heard from. She tried to take that as a good sign. She took several bottles of water from the box in the trailer, shouldered her pack, and stepped out into the sultry night.

Heat from the earth beat her face in waves, and sweat immediately broke out, to be cooled by the brisk, chilly evening breeze that raced down the mountain.

She reached the end of the road. The piles of lava, ropy and bubbled, oozed and dried long ago, met her boot as she took a deep breath and stepped up into the blackness.

The flow was far from silent, and far from empty. Despite her staff's efforts, tourists still milled about. At this point, the lava was old and set, and relatively safe, so long as people didn't go right to the cliff's edge. The gawkers had a party air, like a Fourth of July picnic. They had set up blankets and camp stools, facing the active flow. With each rush of lava or fiery fountain, the crowd oohed and aahed.

They seemed well-behaved to Melanie, and she had too much to think about to play tour-guide. The glow was so bright she didn't need her flashlight, and experience gave her sure-footedness through the darker areas. The temperature rose markedly as she walked farther from the sea and nearer to the geologists. They had moved farther up the shield, and were now observing Kupaianaha itself, the second but now more active of the two vents.

Melanie's stiff, unyielding protective gear was stifling as she struggled up the steep slope towards the scientists.

The burning oranges, yellows and reds of the lava seared through her eyes, into her brain. When she looked down at her footing, she had the disconcerting illusion that her feet ran with flame.

Although she was now near the team, she heard nothing but the crash of molten surf. Noisier than storm surge against rock, it numbed the ears, dulled the senses with its overpowering sound, rushing, pounding, swirling, unceasing.

One coated, helmeted figure squatted near her, writing something. She approached and tapped its shoulder. Nalani Hope, geologist, looked up and waved.

Melanie smiled and squatted next to her. "Howzit? Everything all right?" she yelled into Nalani's ear.

"Yeah! Good!" Nalani yelled back, white smile glowing in her smoke- and soot-darkened face.

"Any change?"

"We gon' lose Royal Gardens dis time."

"Oh, no. For sure?"

"Nothing's for sure. But, yeah. I know."

"Jeez. Everybody's out, yeah?"

"Yeah. And Kapa'au, too. Kalapana Gardens is waiting to hear. The lava's at the top of the subdivision, and it's all downhill now, you know. Maybe we don't lose them all. This time. Who can say?"

"Yeah." Melanie felt tears prick the backs of her eyes at the thought of her friends and family who might lose their homes. Up in flames in minutes. No insurance. She knew the insurance companies didn't insure you if you lived on a volcano. At least, not for eruption. All loss.

She herself lived at the park, but also had a small house in Volcano. That could go, too. Her parents lived in Hilo. They had almost died when the tsunami had hit in the fifties. The house still had a high water mark, eight feet up the dining room wall. They had decided not to repaint. Good to have a reminder not to take too much for granted. Melanie shook herself out of her reverie and shrugged off her pack, handing Nalani a water bottle.

"Thanks."

"What can I do? You guys need anything?"

"Nah. So far, it's okay. But look." She pointed down the shield, and Melanie could see the "party-goers" she had passed hiking up. She wrestled her binocs out of the mass of energy bars in her pack and trained them on the crowd.

"They sure look like they're having fun down there."

"They are. They don't have houses about to burn, I bet."

Melanie lowered the field glasses and saw Nalani's mouth in a hard line. "Somebody you know going to lose his house?"

"My *hanai* uncle's Walter Yamaguchi."

"Oh." *Hanai*—adopted, as in part of the extended family that makes up Hawaiian communities. That was all Melanie needed to hear to conjure up a thousand memories of her family at Yamaguchi's store in Kalapana. As a girl, she'd often gone to visit her cousins, and they'd always ended up at Yamaguchi's General Store—the only store for miles, and you could find the best stuff there! Shave ice in any flavor, fabric, cuttlefish—dried and *hauna* as all get out, but somehow the stink made it an even more appealing snack—*mochi*, Spam *musubi*, toys!

Folks sat out front and talked story. Same folks, everyday. Open, friendly, welcoming tourists and residents alike with their Aloha spirit and homemade leis. Everybody knew everybody's business.

Like the time Melanie and her cousins, Junior and HenryLynn, had climbed the papaya tree in Mrs. Matsuda's yard after she had told them not to. They got a papaya from the bunch twenty feet off the ground, but they dropped it, and it broke her back window. They scrambled down the tree and ran for Auntie Lynn's house—Junior and HenryLynn's mom.

Auntie Lynn didn't seem to know what had happened, but sent them to Yamaguchi's store for sugar. By the time they got there, everyone had heard about the broken window, and Mrs. Matsuda appeared in the doorway threatening paddling and giving them scoldings all the way down the block. They nearly died of shame and had to clean her nasty ol' chicken coop for a month, *plus* pay for the window.

On the shield, Melanie felt a heaviness that wasn't from exhaustion at the thought of so many childhood memories wiped out, along with the Yamaguchis' livelihood.

"I'm sorry, Nalani."

"Yeah, me, too."

"Hey, what's up you guys?" a male voice above them asked.

Melanie creaked upright. "Hi, Dean. Water?" She handed him a bottle and he drained it. "What's the prognosis, doc?"

"The flow is so fast and so heavy it's forced farther east, and it's at the top of Royal Gardens subdivision now."

"Yeah, Nalani was just telling me. Kapaʻau, too?"

"Yeah." He wiped the sweat from his gray, ash-streaked brow with a gloved hand, leaving a white streak, a zebra-like forehead.

"Can we stop it?"

He just looked at her.

"Never mind. I know. Stupid to ask." Melanie trained the binocs on the flow. "So what's next?"

"We just monitor. Keep everyone up on the progress. Get folks the hell out of the way."

"Do you need anything?"

"We're eating in shifts, resting when we can. Right now it's escalating, and I want to be sure Pele doesn't do anything unexpected." The night wind whipped around them, and Melanie shivered, despite her heavy gear. "Tomorrow's gonna be worse, I think."

"Worse? How worse?"

"From what I can tell, were gonna have a shitstorm of reporters. I understand they're already coming in on the Kalapana side. I think every major country is represented, plus some I never heard of. A buncha choppers, photographers, everybody you can think of. Somebody said they saw Tom Brokaw, but I think that's BS."

Melanie's stomach sank with each word. The park had always

dealt with media, particularly when the volcano was active, but this eruptive episode had already been far more destructive than most, and promised to continue. The long-term effects of a media blitz didn't bear thinking about.

"Have you guys seen the HPD training officer lately?"

"Who's that?" Nalani asked.

The geologists had been exempt from the training and had missed the introductions. "K.O. from Honolulu PD. She's here to train the rangers and staff, but I sent her out to roust the permit campers. Seen her?"

"Uh, uh. Anymore water?" Nalani asked.

"Yeah."

"Why would she be down here?"

"Well, she wouldn't, I guess." Melanie handed out more water. "It's just that I sent her out this morning, and no one's seen her since."

"You have a reason to think something's wrong? You been busy, right? Maybe she's in a bar in Hilo, havin' a cold one after a tough day at the office."

"Yeah. Maybe. It doesn't seem like her to just take off."

"You're not exactly available today, are you? Besides, maybe she knows the best thing she can do to help is to get out of the way."

"You're probably right. I got enough to worry about." The orange glow backlit the two geologists as Melanie gave out more water bottles.

A breathless geologist rushed up to Dean. "We got a problem. A couple, maybe."

"Spit it out, man," said Dean.

"The flow's picking up. Volume's increased, and so has pace in the last half hour. Something's gonna blow soon. The lava's pressing more north and east because of the mass. We could get a crossover into the subdivision sooner than we thought. Like tonight."

"Shit. Where?" Dean focused his field glasses in the direction the man pointed. "Okay. I see. What the hell's that?"

"The other problem. Do you see it, too?"

"Is that a person? Out there? Now?" Dean paused between each phrase, disbelief clear in his tone.

"Where?" Both Nalani and Melanie frantically swiveled their own glasses across the flow.

"I think so. I've been watching for a few minutes to be sure. I'm sure. There's more than one. They seem to be running."

"Oh, my god. Right towards Kuapaianaha."

"Oh," Melanie gasped on an indrawn breath. She saw them. Far away, two small figures darted across the black lava, their pattern unsteady, erratic and jagged. The observers could tell what perhaps the runners could not. They were headed straight towards the raging lava flow and its source. Surely they would stop before they reached it, but that was not the only problem.

Vents. Skylights. Thin crust. The figures would see the river. What they could not see lay just below the surface of the cooling lava. The surface of the far field was riddled with deathtraps. Instant immolation in one false step.

Perhaps Pele would get a more substantial sacrifice than the usual ti leaves and gin.

"Get on the radio!" yelled Nalani.

"We're out of range!" Melanie yelled back. "I'll have to hike for help. That could take hours. We can't reach them from anywhere but the north side of the shield. If we hike from here, it will take even longer." She could not tear her eyes away from the bizarre scene playing out a thousand yards of molten rock away. The area was so lit by rioting flame, the black, sexless, featureless figures were clearly visible to the watchers, like shadow puppets.

"No choppers 'til morning," Dean shouted. "Civil Defense banned any night flights since that tour copter got hit by a geyser and went down smoking. This eruption's too unpredictable."

Melanie nodded distractedly, watching in utter disbelief as a third figure ran out onto the far side of the shield. It seemed to follow the first two, although Melanie could no longer see them.

This figure held its arm out, pointing, and Melanie knew, with no factual basis, that it carried a gun.

Her heart pounded with helplessness and despair. She should go for help. She should hike back to Chain of Craters Road and use the radio with the stronger signal at the trailer. She should drive around to the north trail with a team and help. She should . . . do something. But even as she thought of all this, she did not move. Could not move. She watched a sort of dance as two of the people grappled. For the gun? She didn't know. They fell. Rolled down, closer to the brilliant river. Struggled upright. The remaining figure crawled towards the two, pointed, and the couple fell again. Several minutes passed. None of them moved.

"Get up!" she howled and took the glasses away, rubbing her eyes. All the geologists stood transfixed, field glasses trained across the gulf, Pele and her work forgotten, in what Melanie now knew was a life-and-death struggle.

In a flash of insight, she knew one of the players was K.O.. But which one? The tears she'd held back for hours finally streamed out, and she alternately wiped her eyes and the volcanic steam off the glasses. All she could do now was wait. And pray.

CHAPTER THIRTY

The gunshot spurred K.O., and she flattened herself against the cliff, her heart beating wildly, breathing raggedly. A man launched from the opening, and ran erratically down the slope towards a tumble of boulders. K.O. pushed off from the wall and watched him. As he dived behind the pile, a screaming woman appeared in the slit, just feet from where K.O. stood. K.O. could not see her around the wall, but listened to her rant.

"You son of a bitch! I goin' kill you, you know. You one *cop*! A dirty cop, and if I don't get you, Rudy guys will." K.O. heard her heavy breathing, her voice fading in and out as the woman searched for her target. The woman moved away from the cave, down the mountain, and K.O. again flattened herself against the wall, hoping she was invisible in the dark. A glow from the eruption backlit the man, and K.O. saw him risk a look up the mountain. The woman saw him too, for the pile was the only cover for many yards.

Apparently the woman had run out of vocal steam, for although she moved quickly, she neither spoke, nor made much noise as her slippered feet quietly padded along the *paho'eho'e* lava.

K.O. waited until she thought the woman was out of earshot, then cautiously followed. The mountain behind her was in full dark, and she kept the woman between herself and the volcano's eerie glow. As she walked, the sound of pounding surf drifted to her, and she was surprised to hear it up here.

A cop! That was what she had heard. Maybe a dirty cop? If there was any chance the man was a cop, K.O. had to help. Even if he wasn't. Even if *he* was a criminal, K.O. was sure the woman wasn't a cop, and her duty lay in preserving life.

Come up with a plan. Nothing. The woman cautiously approached the mound of tumbled boulders. K.O. slowed, waiting. The man must have escaped. But where to? K.O. let out a breath, not realizing she'd been holding it. The only place he could have gone was down. The woman continued down the slope and K.O. followed slowly, afraid she was making an inordinate amount of noise. True, she couldn't see where she put her feet, but still— She maintained distance as best she could.

She reached the tumble of boulders. On the upslope side, the pile was relatively low, but behind it the mountain sheered sharply away. Her legs went out from under her, and she sat abruptly. She was directly above the entire lava shield, and between Pu'u O'o vent and Kupaianaha. She realized the sound of pounding surf was, in fact, a torrent of lava, spouting, spraying, rushing towards the sea. The speed of it terrified her, and its nearness paralyzed her. Heat rose in waves off the flow, borne by the wind, and sparks flew skyward in the velvet black night. The pulse of the land surged beneath her hands, and she was dimly aware of the heat seeping through her heavy jeans and jacket. Her eyes darted back and forth across the flow, searching for the couple who had so boldly, or stupidly, raced here. She forced herself to look more carefully, and what she saw alarmed her. The flow was not one solid river of lava; it was many. They ran and bobbed, circling rises of cooler lava, dipping into valleys and crevices, to splash up and form one larger stream, only to split again fifty yards farther on.

How could anyone pass through that hell? Or go around it? She saw the man, who dodged and ducked, leaped and twisted, stumbled and lurched. The woman followed ever closer. Sure-footed and fleet, she leapt small streams, skylights and cracks. Her quarry, ever slower, struggled to hide, to flee, to avoid the inevitable incineration.

K.O. trembled, and forced herself upright. *He's a cop,* she told herself. *I have to. Do I really? What is my obligation here? Aid a fellow officer in trouble. Capture a criminal. At the very least, it's attempted murder now, since that woman shot at him. Would I even hesitate if this were a dark alley in Waikiki? Or an abandoned warehouse in Iwilei? Not for a second.* She blinked, and found she was halfway down the shield, picking her way between two large rivers. She stepped cautiously, afraid of crashing through a thin crust and into boiling lava a hundred feet deep.

I wouldn't have to worry for long, she thought. The idea terrified her, so she shut it out. Concentrated on the task at hand. Reminded herself of a call in her early days of patrol—a jumper, a building in Waikiki. Two jumpers, really. Her patrol car had screamed around the corner from Ena Road, and in the driveway of the building she'd seen the bits and pieces of a jumper. Her first. Didn't look human. Not anymore. She had missed him by moments. Whatever his problems had been, they were over. But, there was a second jumper—his lover, depressed and afraid, ready to follow him off the lanai. K.O. had blocked out the sight of the first one. Concentrated on the second. She didn't even remember what she had said. An expert was supposed to come and talk the guy down, but he wasn't there. Up to her. She didn't know what the hell she was doing then. Still, she had succeeded.

She didn't know what the hell she was doing now. But she would focus, all her energy, all her strength on the job at hand.

Getting to the cop, not getting shot, not burning to death. Her advantage was surprise. Neither of these two knew she was there. It gave her strength.

While K.O. had talked herself down to the danger zone, the man had managed to circle north and was now coming towards her. Trapped between two streams of lava, she ducked behind the only large protrusion in range—a large boulder. Immediately her legs spasmed into sharp, excruciating cramps. She tried to remain crouched, but the pain forced her to stretch her legs to relieve them.

It was at this ungraceful moment that the man dodged behind her boulder, a .38 in one hand.

"Shit!" he said.

"Oh, my God!" K.O. said. She immediately saw his bloody arm, but the blood did not appear fresh. She also saw the gun. He pointed it at her.

"What the hell?" he said.

"I came to help," said K.O. "Really. Put that down. I'm on your side."

"What side is that?" His voice was hoarse from running and breathing vog, and K.O. had a hard time understanding him.

"You're a cop, right?"

"Jeez, does everybody know?"

"No. I just heard."

"So what? What the hell are you doing *here?*"

"Long story, but I heard your girlfriend there." K.O. leaned out to see the woman's progress. She was standing, looking at the flow, gun still in hand, about fifty feet away.

"But here! Why? How? Never mind," he said weakly. "Where is she?"

"About fifty feet down, just standing there, you know?" No response. She looked at the man closely. He seemed nearly unconcious. He also looked familiar. Oh, no. That guy from Ocean View. Dealer? *Crap.*

"Hey, brah. Don't go into shock on me, here. Your girlfriend's gonna shoot us both. Give me that." She took the weapon and checked the chambers. Loaded. "Got any more ammunition?" No answer. She peeked again, and saw that the woman was coming towards them now, her face a mask, stony and blank, arm raised, weapon ready. K.O. saw that she no longer wore the rubber flip-flops. How was that possible on the lava? It had hardened, sure, but it was still hot and smoking.

"Hey, you! We gotta go. *Da kine's* coming. Up, brah." K.O. urged him up. He was heavy and sticky. He roused himself enough to help her.

"I los' a lot a blood, man."

"I know, but we gotta go." She risked another look. The woman approached from the north. K.O. would go south. South, however, led to a much narrower finger of black between orange streaks. Thus far, they'd kept anywhere from fifty to a hundred feet from the flow, and that was plenty close as far as K.O. was concerned. No choice. The woman wanted this guy, was willing to get herself killed in taking him down. *Nuts.* K.O. shoved the gun into her waistband and wedged her shoulder under his good arm. They stumbled down the finger of drying lava. It was a dead-end, in all senses of the word. They still had a good lead, but where would that get them now? K.O. had to do something.

"Jolene," the man mumbled.

"What?" K.O. would have to stop the woman any way she could.

"Bitch."

Enough of a clue for K.O. "That your girl back there?"

"Yes. Not my girl. Mark."

"Your name is Mark? I thought it was Gerald or something."

"Gerald, yeah." He opened his eyes and studied her, while she used the moment to breathe and pull the gun from her waistband. She hated having to put it there. *If I were a man, I'd probably shoot my nuts off,* she thought. As it stood, she didn't really want to shoot anything there, anyway. She decided not to pursue the name-thing at the moment. Didn't seem all that important.

"You're the *haole* chick—Jerry's friend, yeah?"

"Yeah. I'm Jerry's friend. K.O. Remember?"

He nodded. "Sorta."

"Don't worry about it. We got worse problems. I'm going to set you down. I might have to shoot your friend, there. She seems determined to shoot one or both of us. Don't need you getting shot again. Getting myself shot would just be the perfect end to a perfect day." As she bent to help him sit on the steep slope, pebbles rolled under their feet and they fell. The weapon discharged, but K.O. managed to hold onto it, as they rolled several yards on the narrowing island.

K.O. looked upslope and saw Jolene lying facedown on the lava, arms outflung.

The surface heat forced K.O. to lift Gerald up again, and she called out.

"Hey, Jolene! Whatever your name is. Get up. It's too hot. Get up!"

Jolene slowly raised her head, and pushed up to hands and knees, gun still clasped tightly in her fist.

"Crap! If she comes after us, I'm gonna have to put you down again. Sorry, brah. We'll catch up later." K.O. was reluctant to put Gerald down on the hot surface.

She heard a muffled *click, click* over the roar of the fire as Jolene crawled closer, the gun hitting the ground with each movement.

"Jolene. I'm a police officer. If you don't stop, I'll shoot."
Click. Click.

"Jolene. I don't want to shoot you. You're already in trouble, don't make it worse. Stop." K.O. held her weapon ready, and realized that she would have to put Gerald down. It seemed that Jolene wanted a physical confrontation, and she couldn't meet it holding up a hundred and eighty pound man.

She was suddenly struck by the absurdity of her situation. How would she explain this to her best friends, Lana and her chief clerk, Selena? For just a flash, a millisecond, K.O. was with them, and that was all Jolene needed. When K.O. let out an involuntary laugh, in that moment, Jolene fired from only yards away.

K.O.—nerves honed to razor edge despite her exhaustion and

fear—also fired. They all collapsed onto the flow.

K.O. felt like her butt was on fire. She opened her eyes, and found her head pillowed on Gerald, but her lower body rested on the flow. Hot. She looked at Gerald. He had fallen when she dived out of the way, a day late and a dollar short, but nonetheless bullethole-less. Her head hurt where it had hit his sternum, but probably a lot less than his head hurt where he had hit rock. The backpack made an uncomfortable bulge under her.

The woman! She sat up quickly and lunged for her gun. "Ai!" The gun was as hot as the inside of an oven. Would the bullets explode? *Great.* Add that onto the day's list of accomplishments. Maybe it wasn't that hot. She used her jacket sleeve to protect her hand and popped open the chamber. Maybe now they wouldn't explode? *Crap.* This wasn't covered in the police academy. She popped out the rounds and frowned as she threw them towards the flow. She didn't want them to explode in her pants. Yet another pretty picture. She carefully set the open revolver in a crevice several feet away. Didn't want either of these idiots to get it, and it was too hot to handle. *Smooth move, Ogden.* Weaponless. Again. She turned her attention to the woman.

Jolene lay on her back, also weaponless. K.O. cautiously approached and looked for the gun. Under her? Jolene's arms were in sight, as well as her hands. Her flowered shirt reflected the bouncing flames, her hair spread like seaweed on the rock. K.O. squatted next to her and felt for a pulse. Faint, but there. Jolene's pale face, the skin finally at rest; the angry, disturbed lines K.O. had seen, now smoothed.

Now what? K.O. wondered. Here I am, the only sane and able person here, and I can't do anything about it. She quickly ran her hands under Jolene's prone body, searching for the gun. Nothing. She pulled Jolene's hands in, and placed them on her stomach, a more restful pose. K.O. had the urge to smooth her brow. That was a little much, she thought, and went back down the slope to Gerald.

"You okay, brah?" K.O. asked.

"I think so. What happened?"

"You mean this last time, or in general?"

A faint smile. "Just this last time."

"Can you sit up, you think? You're not shot. I mean, not again. I can bandage your arm, now." She pulled him up, and he gasped, then breathed a sigh of relief.

"That's damn hot down there."

K.O. smiled and ripped off a piece of his already-ragged shirt, using it to bind his arm firmly.

"Ouch! Man, you're not a nurse, are you? I'd hate to have you in the hospital."

"Nope. Didn't you hear when I tried not to shoot your girlfriend?"

"She's not my girlfriend. Did you shoot her? Is she dead?" His eyes were large in his face, but K.O. could not tell if the woman's death would be a good thing to him or not.

"No. I missed. But she fell and hit her head, so she's out of it. Gives me time to think what to do."

"What do you mean, what to do? Get the hell out of here. What do you think?"

"Take an attitude, brah. Look around you. You're a mess—injured, in shock—lost a lotta blood. She's insane, trying to kill us both. I got no cuffs, no guns, and I don't think the limo's gonna be here anytime soon. What do you think we should do?" She glared at him. He could at least be a little grateful. "I can't pack you both out. No way. Somebody's bound to look for me in the morning. It's safe to say nobody's looking for you, right?"

"Right. Can we at least move up higher? It's so damn hot here, I'm gonna melt. We can take turns guarding her. What do you mean, no cuffs, no guns?"

"Picked right up on that, did you, Sherlock?"

"I have a head injury. Probably."

"Whatever. I'm a police officer. Honolulu PD, and at least I'm not in disgrace. Yet. I may be after this little fiasco."

"I'm not in disgrace, either."

"Whatever." K.O. slung his good arm around her and braced him against her shoulder. She started the long climb to relative safety above this line of seething lava. She was almost used to it. The size, the roar, the heat. Almost. When she paused to rest she said, "Yeah? That's not what I hear. Your crazy woman said you were dirty."

"She was supposed to think that." They huffed upward, slowly, K.O. concentrating on their words so she wouldn't have to think about the flow. Or how close to safety they were. And how far.

"She sounded pretty convinced."

"I've been undercover for over a year, working the marijuana operation that her boss, who is also her cousin, runs."

"Well, for an undercover guy, you didn't cover your tracks very well." They reached a flat spot that K.O. deemed relatively safe. Ten degrees cooler and less chance of the big slip, rolling down until you were a briquette. She shivered at the thought. And the view. She sat next to Gerald. "Now I'm practically cold. It's been forever." She looked at her watch. "Stopped again! I don't believe it." She ran a hand through her hair, and a fistful of broken fibers came off in her hand. "Oh, no."

"What?" She showed him, and now, the tears she had held in trickled out, making tracks in the grime.

"What the hell?" She thought he meant her hair, or her reaction to it, but he was looking down the flow.

"Oh, my God."

Jolene was on her feet, walking towards the southern edge of the lava peninsula, nearing the drop off. K.O. heaved herself up in a rush of adrenaline and ran down the slope. Jolene saw her coming and stopped, two steps from the edge. K.O. saw smoke or steam from around Jolene's bare feet, her shirt almost burned away from her back. Although Jolene had turned to look in her direction, K.O. felt she did not see her. Jolene turned again and faced the lava.

"Tell Rudy I'm sorry. I couldn't do what he wanted. He would kill me, anyway, but I will give myself to you. I've always been with you. I have failed Rudy, my family, but I will not fail you." She took one step.

"Hey! Don't do this." Oh, God. Just like the jumper. She's gonna do it. She doesn't even know I'm here right now. "Please Stop. Rudy will forgive you. I'll make sure he can't hurt you. Hey!" She wasn't getting through.

Jolene slowly raised her arms in supplication. *"E Pele e! Ke akua o ka pohaku enaena, e lawe iaʻu!"*

K.O. knew enough Hawaiian to realize she was hearing a sacrifice. She lunged, but the woman took the last step, and K.O.'s hand clasped only air.

CHAPTER THIRTY-ONE

K.O. never knew how she got back up the slope again to Gerald. Her first recollection was of sobbing, great gasping heaves, against Gerald's good shoulder. Her tears dried almost as soon as she shed them.

"Tell me. What was really going on?" she finally asked him. "Nobody can look for us, assuming they even know I'm here, until morning. There's time. Tell me." She lay back on the now comfortably warm lava and watched, detached as the lava surged and flowed, boiling down the mountain, unaware of the human cargo it carried.

"It started almost two years ago. The drug trade was getting out of hand in the islands. I went into training for a new program— an undercover project. The first step of which was to disgrace myself at Hilo PD. We leaked rumors. I was seen completely drunk and belligerent at local bars. I was supposed to be on the take. All a set-up. All deliberate. In the department, only my lieutenant and the Chief knew. Hilo is a small town; rumors spread quickly. The more people who knew, the more chance of a leak. One I didn't want." His tone had lost the "local-boy" accent and become clipped and professional.

"The hardest part was my family. I couldn't even tell them. I know they looked up to me. My dad was a police officer, died in the line of duty. My brother and I both wanted to be cops. All our lives, we couldn't wait to grow up and be cops. My younger brother Clay failed the medical and couldn't get in. It was up to me. I got in. I'm a twelve-year veteran. It had to seem like I was throwing it all away. I thought it was worth it, to put a major dealer and supplier out of operation." His voice strained a little as he lay back beside her. "Man, this hurts. I guess I'm not gonna die from it, though."

"I just thought of something. Is your brother Clayton Hsu at the park?"

"Yeah. You know him?"

"He's in my training class this week. He's a piece of work."

"I know. I blame myself. He was really proud of me. I hope to put things right. I'm out of the operation, now. I know Jolene told Rudy I double-crossed them. I did. I'm no good to them. I just gotta stay alive."

"Go on, back to the plan. What's this big double-cross?"

"I gotta go back a little farther than that. Okay, we'd set this all up, and it was going great. I was about to get bumped on my ass. Nobody knew how I kept my job, and I was approached, just like I knew I would be. This is a small place; a dirty cop's a good person to have on your team. Plus, I went out of my way to let them know I was available. The first guy they brought in was my friend, Tommy. Tommy was a DEA agent. Deep cover. Started way before me. I was brought in second. Made it more legit."

"Wait. You lost me. You're Hilo PD *and* Drug Enforcement Agency?"

"No. I was acting as an agent for the DEA, assisting them in their program. It was their show. Anyway, I was undercover a little over a year, and thought I was ready to make the bust. It all went to shit when Jolene killed Tommy."

"I didn't expect that," K.O. said sadly. "I'm sorry."

"Yeah. I didn't expect that, either. She murdered him right in front of me. I knew I was in trouble then, that they probably knew more than the story I was leaking. They were supposed to know I was a cop. I didn't tell them. It wasn't anything we discussed over a beer, but it was part of it. Now, I don't know. Two ways to play. One, they knew about Hilo PD, and found out about the DEA connection, or two, they didn't know about the PD, but found out, didn't like it, and the DEA link never came up.

"I've done nothing but think about it since Tommy died. How could I have changed it? Seen it coming? Prevented it? I decided I wasn't going to give up the operation, make Tommy's work, his life—and death—for nothing." He was silent for a few moments.

K.O. opened her eyes and saw his jaw working. "You can cry, you know. You deserve it. After what we've been through tonight" —K.O. took a breath—"maybe we're not gonna get out of here. So, hey, you can cry. If you don't want to cry for that, cry for your friend."

He did, and she held him.

Towards dawn, a helicopter found them, in shock, dehydrated, terrified, but alive, twenty feet from crust only an inch thick.

CHAPTER THIRTY-TWO

K.O. and Gerald were airlifted to Hilo Hospital, and K.O. was released that afternoon. After some antibiotics, fluids, a shower, and clean clothes, she got a ride from Gerald's grateful lieutenant back to Hawai'i Volcanoes National Park.

Gerald remained hospitalized, but in great spirits, since the afternoon paper had carried his heroic story. He was fully credited with the bust of Rudy's operation, since he had been able to make one last drop of a micro-cassette tape with enough evidence to stick.

He was back in the bosom of his family, and the usually morose Clayton arranged a party in his room, the depression and anxiety of the past year lifting off him like a bird on the breeze.

At the barracks, K.O. pushed open the door, bracing herself for a barrage of teen noise, but was greeted by silence. She let the door slam shut, the smack of the wood echoing in the empty room.

Disappointment filled her as she sat on her bunk, hearing in her head the laughter and jokes that once bounced off the metal walls. Her suitcase was where she had left it yesterday morning, open, in disarray from when she rummaged for warm clothes to prepare for the search. Prepare. That was a laugh. Nothing could have prepared her for that.

She ran a hand through her hair and burst into tears again over the broken, burned, chopped hair—a Peter Pan length instead of her shoulder-length red tresses. The color had even seeped out. Along with her hair, Pele had taken her color. She dropped back to lie on her bunk, arm draped over her eyes. That would be bad enough, but Pele also had her eyebrows and eyelashes. "Now, that's just greedy," she complained.

"What is?" asked Melanie.

K.O. sat up. "Melanie!"

Melanie sat beside her and hugged her tight. "I'm so glad you're all right. And that policeman. Quite the revelation in the newspaper!"

"Yeah. Big surprise to me, too."

"Interesting hair."

"Yes. Salon stylings by Pele." K.O.'s eyes were bright with tears. Her skin had a reddish cast, like a bad sunburn, that clashed with her toasted hair.

"That happens a lot around here," said Melanie.

"It does?"

"Yup. These cowboys and cowgirls we call geologists are forever burning something. You'd be amazed how much a good eyebrow pencil goes for around here."

"You're kidding!" K.O. actually laughed. It hurt, but felt good, too.

"Nope. We're gonna fix you up. Then we got plans."

"Plans? What kind of plans?"

"Not telling. Bring your stuff. You're checking out of the Kilauea Hilton, and into a cabin at Volcano House."

"Oh, thank you! I've always wanted to stay there!"

"It's the least we can do. Really, it is the least!" They giggled like girls and gathered her things. K.O. slammed the door one last time, shutting out the voices of teens checking blood sugar, teens combing hair, dressing, pillow fighting. She shut out Angela and

Kimmy, lying hand in hand on the bunk the last time she'd seen them, while she lied to them about being fine, that she knew what she was doing. *I didn't even get to say good-bye.*

In the large restroom at Volcano House, Melanie sat K.O. on a stool, and trimmed her ragged hair. She wouldn't let K.O. look until she'd applied gel, hair spray, and a deftly-wielded eyebrow pencil.

When K.O. looked, she gasped in delight. The face she saw was a far cry from the hollow, burned-out face in the hospital mirror. It was also a far cry from her old self, but that was okay, she decided. *I'm not my old self. I shouldn't look like it. At least, not for a while.*

She laughed at her startled expression, and Melanie adjusted her drawn-on brows to a more relaxed arch. K.O. took the pencil and added a line to her washed-out eyes, still lashless, but made visible with a bit of definition.

She nodded with satisfaction at Melanie's surprisingly stylish cut, long on top, shorter on the back and sides, now spiked up, giving her face a shape her previous style hadn't.

"Now. I'll get your stuff. Get dressed. In something not from the hospital donation pile!" She eyed K.O.'s current ensemble: a loose-fitting, too-short pair of jeans and an "Official Bikini Inspector" T-shirt. "It's time for dinner. You need to relax and have something to eat." Melanie was back in a moment with K.O.'s bag. "Come to the dining room when you're ready."

K.O. opened her duffle to find a new pair of black linen pants, and a bottle-green camp shirt—light, airy, extremely flattering and comfortable on her tight, painful skin. "Melanie!" Tears threatened to well up again at this thoughtfulness, but she firmly repressed them. She didn't want to have to redraw either eye-liner or brows. That thought made her laugh, and she carefully dressed in the lovely garments.

The dining room was nearly empty, since the park had been evacuated. Several staff members ate at various tables, and waved as she passed.

Melanie stood near the windows, looking at the setting sun, over the dark pit of Kilauea Caldera. "There you are. You look great. Your table's this way."

"Thanks. My table? You aren't joining me? And thank you so much for the clothes, they're—oh, I don't know what to say!"

"It wasn't all me. I just helped a little. And no, I'm not joining you. Here you go."

"But I don't want to eat alo—," she started to say, as Melanie sailed off.

"Hi."

"You're—early!" was all K.O. could think to say to the vision before her. Alani. She'd thought of him so often, yet he had been so far away from her thoughts the last twenty-four hours. "Alani! I . . ."

Alani stood and just held her. Gently. Melanie must have told him about her injuries. God! Her hair! Those two must have plotted this. But how?

Who cared? She inhaled deeply, her face fitting perfectly in the curve of his strong neck. His warm skin pulsed beneath her cheek, and his strength filled her. Except for a distinct weakening in her knees, but that was of an entirely different nature. And perfectly acceptable.

"What are you doing here?" she mumbled against him. He pushed her gently away, and seated her.

"What?"

"What are you doing here?"

"I wanted to come early. I also heard on the news what had been happening here at the park. The eruption is the center of the world right now. I had already decided to jump on a plane, and when I got to the park, Melanie told me what happened."

"When did you get here?"

"This morning. I was going to surprise you, but you surprised me first."

"Yeah, well. That wasn't in the plan."

Alani's rich, deep laugh rumbled out, and K.O. gulped her water to hide her discomfort. It would have worked, too, if she had not swallowed so much and had a coughing fit.

"I was all ready to rush to the hospital to be by your side, when Melanie told me you were getting out and came up with a better plan."

K.O. saw the twinkle in his eye. "Thank you so much for the clothes. You did it, right?"

"Melanie and I did it together. I guess clothes are a kind of intimate gift, and I wasn't sure how you would take it. So we cooperated."

I'll tell you how I'll take it, K.O. thought, absorbing his beautiful brown eyes, his expressive hands, the few curling black hairs poking out of the vee of his shirt.

"Do you know what you want?"

"Absolutely!" K.O. said breathlessly. Then cringed. A waitress stood at her elbow. "House salad. And lots of your delicious bread. Thanks."

"Would you like some wine?" Alani asked.

"I'm on meds, so I'd better not." *I don't need wine.* "'I get no kick from champagne,'" she hummed.

They spent the next hour eating and catching up. K.O., self-conscious at first, eventually relaxed. He still didn't see her, she realized, at least not physically. He saw inside her. Just the way he had when they'd first met, years ago. That was one reason she'd stopped seeing him. It had unnerved her to be so thoroughly understood. Not judged, but just *known.* No one had done that before.

Now she felt ready to be seen. Understood. She wondered if she could see him in the same way. He wasn't perfect. He had slightly crooked teeth, white as beach sand, in a long jaw. Thick, dark, wavy hair. Big brown eyes. Large hands, paddlers hands. Actually, now that she evaluated him, maybe he was perfect.

"What are you doing?"

"What?"

"I asked you what you were doing?" Alani repeated. "I asked you something, and you're staring. Are you okay?" Alarm in his voice. "You're not hurt or in pain, are you?"

You gotta love a man who thinks about you first, K.O. mused. "I'm fine. Just thinking. And I guess I'm a little tired."

Melanie chose that moment to drop K.O.'s cabin key on the table. "Dinner's on me, kids." She turned to Alani. "Nice to meet you. Thanks for the conspiracy."

Alani laughed. "Same here. I'm going to get her to bed. Well, you know."

"Yeah, I know. K.O., don't leave before you say good-bye. Okay?"

"Okay. Thanks, Melanie, for everything." K.O. was suddenly overwhelmingly tired.

"Let's go," said Alani. He picked up her bag in one hand, and put his other arm around her shoulders, warm and comfortingly solid across her back. She leaned into him while they walked the short distance to the cabins.

"I'm right next door to you, connecting room, if you need anything. Okay?"

K.O. was too exhausted to answer. She just nodded. Alani opened her door, set her bag inside, and flicked on the light. She briefly took in a four-poster double bed, a fireplace, a bathroom door ajar, and a second door that must open to the connecting room. She staggered to the bed.

"Hey, whoa. Careful, there," Alani said. He pulled down the covers, and she fell onto the bed.

"Stay," was all she remembered saying.

When she woke up, he was there. Still fully clothed, lying next to her, holding her in the curve of his body, safe and protected. She drifted off to sleep again, pressing his hand to her cheek, feeling his lips on her hair.

CHAPTER THIRTY-THREE

Selena Wade, K.O.'s chief clerk and best friend, picked her up at the Honolulu airport.

"Thanks so much, Selena. How are the kittens doing?" K.O. settled carefully in the front seat and buckled up.

"They are terrifying. Mama Teresa is fine, and we both can't wait until you find them homes. Lana and Lance said they'd take two to christen their new house."

Lana and Lance. K.O. smiled. Alani's sister, her dear friend, had just married an assistant DA.

"The only catch is," Selena continued, as she pulled onto the freeway, "you have to keep them all until they get back from their honeymoon, so they can choose."

"They're still a little young to be adopted out, don't you think?"

"No, I don't." Selena flipped her strawberry-blonde hair out of her face as she negotiated the incredibly short ramp from the H-1 onto the Likelike Highway. "Stupid! I am in this lane, brah!" she yelled and accelerated past a rustmobile.

K.O. smiled and let her head flop back onto the headrest. "Anything new going on?"

"Nah. We go to Evidence at the end of the week. Baker's assigned permanently to Records." K.O. heard the smirk in her voice. "He won't annoy us anymore."

They passed the Kam IV housing project and began the ascent to the tunnels. Walls of tropical foliage were broken by flashes of homes and an occasional church.

"I'll be glad to do something new."

"Yeah, me too." They rode in silence for several minutes. "So, K.O., tell me what happened. I only know what I read in the paper." Selena's voice was gentle.

Haltingly at first, then more firmly, K.O. caught Selena up on the events of the previous week.

"When I woke up the next morning, Alani was still there," she marveled.

"Don't sound so surprised. I knew you guys had something special."

K.O. smiled. "Yeah. We'll see what happens now. Anyway, we stayed at HVNP that day, and I rested, then told everyone goodbye. I signed off the training certificates. After that hell, they totally deserved them. Pele gave them more experience than I ever could.

"We saw Jerry's play. A dress tech rehearsal of 'Deathtrap.' It was really good. Even the girl was amazing. Jerry always had good casting instincts. He about had a heart attack getting this one up and running. The next day we drove to see Alani's friends and relatives in Captain Cook, and then went on to Kona. It was nice. He was so sweet—let me call the shots, always asked if something was too much for me."

"He's a keeper."

"Yeah."

"Don't sound so excited."

"I'm just not used to it, I guess."

"Used to it or not, you deserve it. *Get* used to it!"

"Yeah." K.O. fell silent, remembering the two days alone with Alani, driving around the island, talking, being together. Comforting and comfortable, but tinged with the excitement of attraction, not knowing where it would lead.

"What happened with that *go-yen* necklace? Who had the other one?"

"Gerald Hsu lost his on the wash. I'd seen Clayton Hsu's around his neck at the training sessions. I didn't associate them until it was all over."

Silence as they rode the grade.

"So, that's it?"

"What else? I think I've told you everything."

"You never got to see the kids again? That was so bizarre how that one girl . . .

"Angela."

"Yeah, how Angela just knew."

"Get a grip. There's probably more to it than I know."

"But you didn't get to say good-bye. That's sad."

"I did forget to mention one thing. I didn't get to say goodbye, but Angela and Kimmy and Jane all wrote me notes, and stashed them in my luggage before they went."

"I bet Angela knew from the start." Selena started doing the Twilight Zone music.

K.O. smacked her lightly. "Stop that."

"What did the notes say?"

"Just good-bye stuff. 'Good to meet you.' Jane wants to have lunch sometime after we get settled from all this. She's at Queen's Hospital. Right around the corner."

"But you won't call her."

"I don't know. I'd like to. I think I need more time and distance before I run through it all again."

"Just say you don't want to talk about it."

"It's not that simple."

"I know. Here we are." Selena pulled K.O.'s car into the space at the condo on the windward side of the island. She grabbed K.O.'s bag and locked the car as K.O. slowly ascended the stairs to her second floor unit.

She slipped off her shoes and stepped onto the cool tiles. Expecting the usual contemplative atmosphere, K.O. was shocked to discover the place had been rearranged in her absence. She heard crashing and skittering that stopped moments after the door clicked shut. She raised questioning eyebrows at Selena, who shrugged and moved past her with the duffle bag.

"What the hell happened to my condo?" K.O. finally managed to ask, seeing unidentifiable shards, chips, scraps of paper and the remains of her ti plant. Teresa, her beautiful, striped tabby coat glistening, stepped to K.O.'s side. She stood on her hind legs, patted K.O.'s thigh, and chirruped, the way she did to her kittens. A definite welcome, but accented with typical feline disapproval at K.O.'s absence.

"Teresa." K.O. bent and picked her up, feeling her solid weight and smooth muscle. "She's looking so good, Selena. Thank you. You took such good care of her. She's gained weight and doesn't have that urchin look anymore." K.O. had rescued the abandoned mother and her tiny kittens, a few weeks before, from a den under the red ginger bushes behind the carport. Teresa had decided to stay.

Selena flopped into a recliner in the living room. "You're welcome. Can I crash here tonight and go home tomorrow? I'm pooped."

"Sure." K.O. nuzzled Teresa and settled into the second recliner. Teresa purred audibly, and K.O. felt the vibration through her collar bone and into her chest, warming and soothing her. She began to relax.

A sudden crash jolted all three of them. A flurry of small bodies rocketed out of the guest bedroom and screeched around the tile to the guest bath. A thump signaled that someone hadn't made the turn.

K.O. wearily closed her eyes again. Teresa's rumbling purr restarted. "Is that what it's been like?"

"Twenty-four seven. Starting the second day. The first day, I guess I was a stranger, but they got over that. They're not too coordinated. The first day they broke that hideous tiki thing Abby and Richard bought for you."

K.O. smiled, remembering her mother's elderly, bridge-playing friends who'd visited the islands a few weeks earlier. She'd had no warning they were coming, and her mother had told them K.O. would be at their disposal as a tour guide. She'd ended up taking them, along with her friend Lana, to a tourist luau which had turned out to be fun, although she would never admit it. In thanks, Abby and Richard had given her a cheap tourist tiki two feet high, purchased at a Waikiki stand. It was like no local tiki K.O. had ever seen, with bulging jeweled eyes and potbelly, and too many undefined appendages. Sort of a cross between Mr. Magoo and Kali, an Indonesian goddess, she thought. In fact, K.O. had called it Mrs. Magoo, and hadn't had the heart to throw it away.

"Gee, that's too bad," K.O. murmured to Teresa.

"Yeah, I thought so. But I took it as a sign of impending doom, and put your other stuff in a box in your closet. I didn't have time to pack or wrap them, being busy cleaning up all the other stuff."

K.O. opened her eyes. "What other stuff?"

"Did you know a litter box is just a big playground with homemade toys?"

K.O. snorted and started to laugh.

"Sure. Laugh now. It's your turn next."

K.O.'s laughter faded, and she stroked Teresa, listening to the sounds of kittens at play. Or demolition. She was suddenly overwhelmingly tired.

"I'm going to bed. Don't wake me for dinner, okay? Let's have breakfast together before we go in."

"In where?"

"To work. You do work, remember?" Selena opened her mouth to reply, but K.O. cut her off. "Oh, wait. I know you *go* there, but *work* . . . hmmm. Sorry, my mistake."

Selena tossed a throw pillow at K.O. smacking her in the head.

"That's all the thanks I get."

"No. You have all my thanks." K.O. gently moved Teresa and pushed herself up. "G'night."

"You don't have to report tomorrow. You know that, don't you?"

"I know that. But I want to. We have a whole new department to train to our eccentricities and perfection."

Selena smiled and nodded, chin in hand.

K.O. heard the TV go on as she closed her bedroom door. Teresa had slipped in with her and settled herself in her usual spot, the pillow next to K.O.'s.

K.O. pulled on her current favorite sleeping T and flannel pj bottoms, wincing as they touched her tight skin and tender muscles. She felt emotionally raw as well, and hoped that would fade along with the burns and bruises.

A piece of paper fluttered to the floor from her bag. Angela's note. She picked it up, settled against her pillows, blankets high, and slowly unfolded it, reading once again, the words that could not possibly have come from a little girl.

Dear K.O.:

Know this. You could not have prevented the sacrifice. It was her path to choose, not your path to change. Your path is a challenge, but of your choosing. Trust that what you do is far-reaching and meant to be. All will be well with you, although you do not allow yourself to know it now, where you are.

I won't see you again, but I want you to know that I am thinking of you, and should you need me, I am here.

It was signed only with what looked like a scripted A with ash spiraling from the peak. K.O. fell asleep with the note still in her hand, Teresa's slitted eyes and solid body keeping watch in the darkening room.

The End.

ABOUT THE AUTHOR

Victoria Heckman is the award-winning author of the *K.O.'d in Hawai'i Mystery Series*. The first book in this series, *K.O.'d in Honolulu,* is available from Writers Exchange E Publishing. She is working on the third, *K.O.'d in Hawaiian Sovereignty.* Her short fiction has appeared in *FUTURES, Short Story, Kid's Highway, Mysterical-e, The Smog, Without a Clue, LoveWords, TRUE SOUL MATES, MORE SLOW DEATH,* and *AND SOME OF THEM ARE DEAD,* and she has published numerous articles and newsletters. She has edited two anthologies, co-edited a third, and is a free-lance editor. She is the president of Sisters in Crime-Central Coast Chapter, and is a member of Sisters in Crime National's E Publishing Committee, Mystery Writers of America and the Police Writers Association.

Ms. Heckman divides her time between California and Hawai'i.